"Dash it, Pris!

"I must be when you speak in circles. I wish to speak plainly."

"As I do." Neville put his boot on the bench beside her. Resting his elbow on his knee, he smiled at her. "To own the truth, I would rather not speak at all."

She gazed up into his dark eyes, which were as mysterious as the night. Within them were regions she did not yet dare to explore, but the very thought sent a thrill cascading through her. She laced her fingers through his as he set his glass on the wide sill. Taking hers, he put it beside his before drawing her to her feet.

His arm encircled her waist and drew her against him. His other hand cupped her chin. He tilted it back so she could not evade the powerful emotions in his eyes. She did not want to evade them. She wanted to revel in them, sharing each one. As his thumb moved along her jaw, he smiled.

"Pris." His rough voice when he spoke her name was as gentle as his fingertip tracing her cheek. He whispered her name again before his mouth caressed hers.

With a moan, she gave herself to the kiss. His tongue slipped along her lips, and she delved her own deep within his mouth. Her fingers tightened on his coat as every inch of her begged her to forget they had yet to speak their marriage vows.

He must have been thinking much the same because he raised his head and whispered, "Haven't I told you there is only so much a man can endure?"

Other Zebra romances by Jo Ann Ferguson

DIGGING UP TROUBLE

JO ANN FERGUSON

ZEBRA BOOKS
Kensington Publishing Corp.
http://www.kensingtonbooks.com

For Terri Brisbin
who knows how much trouble we
can dig up in bookstores

ZEBRA BOOKS are published by

Kensington Publishing Corp.
850 Third Avenue
New York, NY 10022

All Kensington titles, imprints and distributed lines are avail-
able at special quantity discounts for bulk purchases for sales
promotion, premiums, fund-raising, educational or institu-
tional use.

Special book excerpts or customized printings can also be created to fit specific needs. For details, write or phone the office
of the Kensington Special Sales Manager: Kensington Publishing Corp., 850 Third Avenue, New York, NY 10022. Attn.
Special Sales Department. Phone: 1-800-221-2647.

Zebra and the Z logo Reg. U.S. Pat. & TM Off.

First Printing: March 2004
10 9 8 7 6 5 4 3 2

Printed in the United States of America

PROLOGUE

It had to be done carefully. Too little weight, and the body could float back to the surface and be found. Too much weight, and it would sink so fast that a storm could rip it from the shallows and wash it up on the shore. This body must never been found, not by fishermen or smugglers or wreckers.

Kneeling down, the man added another stone atop the corpse. He stood and motioned for his comrades to tie the fabric around it. He smiled. Not everyone had a canvas burial shroud.

"Go ahead," he ordered.

The men rolled the body onto a sledge and dragged it toward the sea. The waves were breaking higher than usual tonight, so they needed to take it into deep water. Wind howled around the rocks and into the caves where the sea tried to dig more deeply with every surge.

He watched them haul the corpse into the sea. It was dumped without ceremony, and the men were laughing and joking as they emerged back onto the shore. And why not? They had done the same thing every time someone tried to halt their work or a ship was lured close to the shore in hopes of it breaking up on the rocks so they could claim its cargo.

The men's voices vanished along the shore as they

went to one of the few places where the cliffs could be scaled. He was left alone on the shore with the wind's cries and the sea's frantic song.

He had watched many other bodies given to the sea. It was the way of the shore. There were those who profited, and there were those who paid. Turning, the man walked along the shore. At the base of the cliff where a narrow path was visible only to the most discerning eye, he paused and looked back out to sea.

"You have served me well as an example of what happens to those who betray me." He laughed, the sound swirling in the high wind. "Don't worry about being lonely. Many have gone before you." He looked at the house standing above the cliffs, its four towers at the corners an ebony bulk against the night sky. "And, unless he is wise enough to heed my warnings, there soon will be another to follow you."

ONE

Trouble was easy to find. How many times had Lady Priscilla Flanders said those very words to her children? Now her aunt was saying the same thing to her.

"But I am not looking for trouble," Priscilla answered, grabbing the seat as the carriage bounced into another chuckhole.

Her aunt poked one hand out from under the blankets wrapped around her. "Coming to Cornwall in the middle of winter is asking for trouble."

"I offered to help prepare the house for—"

Pushing back the cocoon of blankets, Cordelia Emberley Smith Gray Dexter wagged her finger at Priscilla. "That is another thing. Whoever heard of holding a betrothal ball at a house at the far end of the island in the middle of winter?"

Priscilla saw her two daughters grinning, although they became as somber as undertakers when their great-aunt glanced at them. She must not let her aunt see her amusement either. Aunt Cordelia was the matriarch of the family, and she could see no reason why her every suggestion should not be obeyed. And obeyed posthaste. Her aunt's hair had not a hint of silver, but she was reputed to cause the graying of many of those around her who were not as accustomed to her ways as Priscilla was.

"Aunt Cordelia," she said in her calmest tones, "you know Neville wishes to use Shadows Fall for our betrothal ball."

"Nonsense. Pure and complete nonsense."

Arguing when her aunt was in such a pelter would be silly, so Priscilla did not attempt it. Instead she smiled at her daughters. Daphne had been surprisingly willing to miss the beginning of the Season, which would be her first. Mayhap it was as simple as the fact that her eldest did not want to chance Priscilla changing her mind about firing her off. Like her older sister, Leah had inherited Priscilla's blond hair. Unlike her older sister, Leah's was mussed. The girl, who would be celebrating her thirteenth birthday a week after the betrothal ball was to be held, always looked as if she had just escaped from a wrestling match.

"I trust you are ready to work," Priscilla said.

Leah nodded. "Didn't Uncle Neville write that we could go through the house and decide which furniture we wanted for our own private rooms?"

"He mentioned that you would probably find your rooms lacking."

Aunt Cordelia muttered something Priscilla did not ask her to repeat.

"This could be a treasure hunt," Leah continued, not letting her great-aunt's reaction discourage her. "Won't it be fun, Daphne?"

"It should be an excellent venue for Mama to teach us about how furniture should be arranged."

Priscilla restrained herself from rolling her eyes. When Daphne took on what her daughter considered her adult voice, it was aimed at trying to prove Daphne was mature enough to attend the upcoming Season.

"Shall we wait," Priscilla asked, "and see the house before you take it upon yourselves to redo all of it? I am certain Neville will have some ideas of his own."

"Which you should not encourage," Aunt Cordelia said. "A wife should be in charge of her home, not the husband. Allow him to believe he is helping, if you must, but do not indulge him."

"I have been married before."

"To a clergyman." Her aunt's nose wrinkled. "Now you are marrying a rogue."

"If you became better acquainted with Neville—"

"I know him well enough."

Priscilla relented again, although every instinct urged her to defend Neville. Her betrothed and her aunt never saw eye-to-eye, in spite of Neville's uncharacteristic attempts at subduing his customary nature. He had hoped to allay her aunt's misgivings when they last spoke in Bath before he returned to London, but Aunt Cordelia continued to view him as an incorrigible troublemaker.

The carriage bounced again, and the girls squealed and giggled. It was just as well that her son Isaac was at school. He would be calling up to the coachee to hit every hole along the road.

She looked out the window. The lights from the village they had passed through had vanished behind them. A stiff wind off the sea kept fog from forming. She was grateful because, before the sun set, she had seen sharp cliffs dropping down to narrow beaches. Branches from thick, gnarled hedgerows reached into the road and occasionally struck the carriage.

When Neville had told her that his family's dirty acres were in Cornwall, she had not been surprised. Such a wild and distant shire seemed to fit what she had heard of the Hathaway family. Neville was the last of his line, for he had inherited his title from a distant relative, raising him from a life in the theater and the darker elements of London to become Sir Neville Hathaway. In the past decade, he had enjoyed his inheritance and tweaking the noses of those in the *ton* who could not hide their curiosity about his past.

Aunt Cordelia was one who never questioned his background. She was thoroughly assured of her opinions that Neville, in spite of his title, was unworthy of any sort of relationship with her niece and her great-nieces and great-nephew.

Priscilla leaned back against the seat as the carriage went down a steep road. She had offered to ride backward in hopes of assuaging her aunt's dismay about this long, cold journey, but it appeared nothing could change Aunt Cordelia's mind about coming to Cornwall or persuading Priscilla to break her betrothal.

If they passed through the gate Neville had told her to look for, Priscilla did not see it. The coachman must have because the carriage slowed and made a sharp turn. No sign of a house was visible, even when the carriage halted. Only when a carriage lantern was taken down as the door was opened could she see an ancient stone wall across a surprisingly wide drive.

Stepping out of the carriage, Priscilla took the lantern. The light did not reach far through the night, although moonlight frosted the tops of the trees crowding the drive. The wind was damp and refused to be stopped by her cloak. It rushed past with a fierceness that battered her ears. Either rain or spray from the sea struck her face. She was unsure how close the house was to the cliffs. On the morrow, she would explore. Tonight, she wanted only to get her family and servants in out of the cold.

With her arm around Leah's shoulders, she led the way up the half-dozen steps to what appeared to be the front door. No lamps were lit, and no windows offered any glow from within.

"Are you certain this is the right house?" asked Daphne from behind her.

"We have followed the directions Neville sent to us."

Aunt Cordelia sniffed. "Doing that was your latest mistake, Priscilla."

This time, Priscilla gave herself the luxury of rolling her eyes. Aunt Cordelia would not be able to see, and such a reaction allowed Priscilla to curb her tongue. Her aunt meant well, but could not disabuse herself of the notion that Priscilla marrying Neville was a very mistaken thing.

Nobody opened the door to welcome them into Shadows Fall. Reaching for the knocker, which was shaped like a ship, she was startled when the door came ajar. It must not have been latched.

Pushing it aside, she went into the house. Damp and odors of the most unpleasant sort almost convinced her to turn around and leave. She breathed shallowly as she held up the carriage lantern to discover the entry hall was an exact circle. That was the only thing perfect about it. At each of the trio of interior doorways opening from it, doors hung drunkenly by a single hinge. Crates were stacked against one arc. From another, a somber portrait glowered at them. Overhead, the ceiling appeared to be cracked, and a series of holes looked as if someone had walked right through the plaster.

"This must be the wrong house," Aunt Cordelia announced, holding her cloak over her nose. "No one in his right mind would consider holding a gathering here."

"But you think Uncle Neville is not in his right mind."
Leah giggled.

Priscilla said, "That is quite enough, Leah." Going to
the portrait of a man holding a white and gold cat, she
peered at the brass plate nailed to the bottom of the
frame. She could not make out the first name even
when she held the lantern close to it, but the last one
was Hathaway. "This must be the correct place."

"But the house appears deserted," argued Aunt
Cordelia.

For once, Priscilla had to agree wholeheartedly with
her aunt. Some light came through the holes in the ceiling, but it might be just moonlight.

"Oh, sweet saints!"

Priscilla whirled, shocked, for her aunt used that expression only when greatly upset. "What is it, Aunt
Cordelia?"

"Blood! On the floor!"

"Blood?"

Leah choked back a gasp and clutched her sister's
arm with one hand and Priscilla's with the other. As her
daughter's fingers dug into her arm, Priscilla stared at
the crimson drops on the floor. Another fell and
splashed, flinging red spots across the stone.

Fell?

Priscilla disentangled her arm from her younger
daughter's fingers. Edging around the red drops, she
looked up. Directly overhead were several holes. She
jumped back as more red cascaded through them.

Holding the lantern high, she climbed the stairs,
which were dotted with small pawprints. The risers were
steady and without a creak. Even so, the sound of her
footfalls must have reached the upper floor before she
did because a long shadow rose to drape across the ban-

ister. Her arm was grasped again, and she saw her daughters had followed her.

"We should leave, Mama," urged Daphne. "If someone is dead up here . . ." She choked back a gasp when the shadow shifted, changing its shape.

"But what if it is Uncle Neville who is hurt?" moaned Leah. "What if someone came in here and attacked everyone?"

"Don't let your imaginations frighten you," Priscilla said. Usually it was her son who had such morbid ideas. "Hush and stay here." Climbing a few more steps, she looked back to see that her daughters had obeyed. They must be very frightened to acquiesce without a single protest.

She went around the top of the banister and along a gallery where a half-dozen more portraits—each as somber as the one below—were hung. She did not slow her pace to examine them. Up here, the air was fresher. A crisp chill suggested a window was open—or broken—nearby. She strode toward the shadow.

As it approached her, she said, "Really, Neville, you could be more careful when you are splashing paint around. Aunt Cordelia nearly suffered from apoplexy when she saw the blood red drops."

A single lamp was lit at the end of the gallery, but it was enough to shine a bluish sheen on Neville's ebony hair. The sharp lines of his face were emphasized by light and shadows across it. Without his coat and waistcoat, his shoulders appeared even broader.

She admired his easy strength as he walked toward her. Spots of crimson splattered his white shirt and breeches, a sight that would have been devastating if she had not seen the paintbrush and bucket he carried. The wall behind him shone with fresh paint.

Neville set the bucket on the floor and took her hand. He did not step closer as he looked down at the front of himself. "Think how much more distressed your aunt would be to see matching spots on us."

"She would swoon right away." Her smile negated her stiff tone. "I believe you owe her an apology."

"For working on my own house?"

She laughed. "That she will find even more distressing than what she thought was blood. She will demand—"

"Why are you painting this wall?" asked Aunt Cordelia as if on cue. "Don't you have servants for such things and to clean up whatever is reeking in this house? And where is your man at the door?"

Neville bowed his head toward her. "Lady Cordelia, I was just about to explain to Priscilla that, once the sun set, I did not expect you to arrive until tomorrow. I believed you to be wise enough to know that one should not traverse these shore roads on a moonless night."

"Was it any more dangerous than staying at a low tavern where smugglers gather?" asked Priscilla, vexed that he was chiding her when she had not seen him in almost a month.

"There, they would be polite to you. If they thought you were spying upon their illegal antics, they would be far less forgiving."

"Are there many smugglers here?" asked Leah eagerly.

He smiled. "Who knows? They don't announce their numbers. However, there are several deep caves along the shore. Where there are caves by the sea, there are smugglers."

"Must you betwattle the child with absurd tales?" asked Aunt Cordelia. "Few smugglers come this far north. Those low creatures prefer St. Ives Bay and Mount Bay."

"I had no idea you were such an expert on the subject of smugglers," Priscilla said, amazed.

"One hears what one hears." She touched the upper banister and grimaced. "I do trust there is a place where we might rest from our sojourn that is not malodorous and filthy."

"Of course." Neville put two fingers in his mouth and whistled even more loudly than the wind. With a smile, he said, "Excuse the primitive conditions, Lady Cordelia, but I have found this the most expedient way to call the servants."

"Have you no bells?"

"I have one. And I have had it put in your room, which you will find clean and refreshed."

"Thank you," Aunt Cordelia said, rather grudgingly. "If you can have us shown to our rooms . . ."

Stoddard, the butler from Neville's house on Berkeley Square, rushed along the gallery. The white-haired man came to a quick stop, almost falling over when he saw Neville was not alone. Dipping his head, he said, "Lady Priscilla, I was not informed you and your family had arrived."

"Please alert the rest of the household that our guests are here," Neville replied, a smile teasing his lips.

Priscilla had sympathy for the butler, whose employment Neville had inherited along with this estate and the house in London. Stoddard always was the pattern-card of kindness to her, although she suspected it was because the butler hoped she would have a civilizing effect on Neville. Even here at Shadows Fall, Stoddard wore his perfectly pressed dark blue livery, clearly not willing to lower his standards.

"Stoddard," she said, drawing off her gloves, "we hope our late arrival will not create too many problems for you and Mrs. Crosby."

"Of course not, my lady. We have everything ready for you." He glanced over his shoulder, and she saw Mrs. Crosby approaching. The housekeeper was settling her cap in place, warning that she had been ready to end her day.

"Good evening, Mrs. Crosby," Priscilla said.

"Welcome to Shadows Fall, my lady, Miss Flanders, Miss Leah." She gave a quick curtsy. "Lady Cordelia."

Priscilla smiled. Neville had instructed his household on everyone traveling with her as well as telling his housekeeper that Aunt Cordelia should be treated with special deference. She hope this augured well for a good visit at Shadows Fall.

"Shall I show the ladies to their chambers, Sir Neville?" the housekeeper asked.

He shook his head. "I will do that. Please have the beds rewarmed, and send someone to guide Lady Priscilla's carriage to the barns." He looked at her daughters. "Are you hungry?"

"Famished!" Leah said, rubbing her stomach.

"Then, Mrs. Crosby, please have the kitchen send up a tray with something to keep this young lady from starving before dawn."

The housekeeper smiled. "It will be brought to your room right away, Miss Leah."

As the butler and the housekeeper went to set the other servants to their tasks, Neville motioned toward the staircase. "A good host would show you to your rooms now so you might have a good night's rest after your long trip. If you please, ladies . . ."

Priscilla was glad when Aunt Cordelia went without

comment. She wondered if her aunt was still upset about the red paint or embarrassed by her reaction to it or just exhausted.

When she started to follow, Neville put his hand on her arm. A thrill surged through her as it did each time he touched her. Had the others disappeared along the gallery, or was her eager heartbeat drowning out the sound of their voices?

"Are you crazy?" he demanded as he took the lantern and, blowing out the light within, set it on the floor.

She stared at him. This was not the profession of affection she had anticipated hearing from him after so many weeks apart. "Mayhap," she returned tartly. "Do you have a reason to ask other than the fact that I accepted your proposal?"

He chuckled. "It sounds as if your good aunt has been outlining the reasons why you were foolish to do so."

"All the way from Bath." Walking with him along the gallery toward where a pair of Chinese vases were crowded together in a niche, she asked, "Do you have another reason for asking if I am mad?"

"Just the same one."

"About our betrothal?" Her steps faltered.

"Certainly not." He put his arm around her waist and drew her closer. "I leave such thoughts to your aunt. My thoughts were aimed more at your well-being when you drive along a shore road after dark."

"The moon was high, which is not the preferred time for smugglers to be about their illegal business."

His fingers caressed her side, but his voice remained stern. "What you and your aunt are assuming about Cornish seamen could get you into trouble. Smugglers haunt every inch of these shores. A moonless night might be their favorite, but they are willing to conduct their trade whenever they can. And wreckers prefer well-lit nights after stormy days to scavenge from the rocks."

"I am impressed with your knowledge of smugglers, too, Neville."

"Is that all that impresses you?"

She smiled. "Just because we are overlooking the sea does not mean you need to fish for compliments."

Leading her up another flight of stairs, these not as wide as the lower ones, he said, "I had hoped my painting skills would impress you."

"Are you aspiring to be Michelangelo?"

"No." He looked up at the ceiling more than fifteen feet above their heads. "Just the walls will be enough to keep me and a half-score of footmen busy for many weeks to come."

"I trust if you paint any other areas with that red, you will warn me so I can make sure Aunt Cordelia is not distressed as she was when she saw it on the entry's floor."

"The entry?"

She smiled. "It was leaking through the holes in the ceiling. You should take more care where you splash paint."

"I was. There must be a hole in that old bucket."

"A good excuse."

With another chuckle as they reached the top of the stairs, he steered her toward the right. The floor was bare, and there was no furniture set between the doors. On the walls more portraits peered out from the shadows.

"Your ancestors were fond of having pictures of themselves, weren't they?" she asked, pausing to look at a dour woman who appeared as if she had never smiled once in her many years. Like the man in the foyer, she held a cat, but this one had a black patch around one eye and on its nose. She wore a pearl and sapphire ring on the fourth finger of her left hand. Looking at several of the other pictures, she saw an identical ring on each woman's hand. It must have been an heirloom that passed from mother to daughter. She wondered when it had been lost or sold.

"Apparently they were so busy posing for portraits that they did not concern themselves with making sure there were future generations to sit for more pictures. I am all that is left of the Hathaways." He gave her a rakish leer. "At least for now."

Priscilla was about to give him an answer as earthy as his comments, for she never minced words with Neville, but paused when she heard her daughters' voices coming from an open doorway. "They are chattering with excitement, so I suppose they are pleased with the rooms you have selected for them."

"Room." He held up a single finger. "As you have seen, the house is in poor condition. It is in worse shape than I had guessed from the reports, so I considered myself fortunate to find a room for your aunt and a room for you and Daphne and Leah."

"Three rooms should be plenty until the rest of my household arrives."

"Two rooms, Pris. One for your aunt, and one for the rest of you. I am afraid you will be quite crowded tonight. By the morrow, I have been assured by Mrs. Crosby, several other rooms will be usable." He ran his finger along her chin. "Of course if you would rather not sleep with your daughters, I could make other arrangements."

She smiled and wrapped her hand around his finger. "Such thoughts will send Aunt Cordelia straight back to Bath."

"All the more reason to think such things."

"Don't let her hear you say that."

He pointed to a closed door. "I doubt if she has her ear pressed to the wood to catch our conversation. She believes me dissipated past redemption."

"And has even less hope for me at this point." She laughed. "She is certain you have led this family down the road to ruin."

"Which I have."

"Most undoubtedly."

Cupping her chin with his paint-speckled hand, he said, "I have missed you, Pris."

"I noticed how much you have missed me by the number of times you wrote to me." She tapped her cheek. "Now, let me see. How many letters did I receive? Oh, yes. One."

He laughed. "You know I am not a man who is accustomed to committing much to writing. What one puts on paper one can be held accountable for at a later time."

"What do you wish not to be accountable for to me?"

"Not you, Pris." He glanced toward the door where her aunt could be heard ringing for a maid. "Yon virago would gladly see me hanged for a single wrong word."

"Hanged? No." She laughed. "Tarred and feathered. Neville, I do hope the two of you can reach a truce."

"You are endlessly optimistic, Pris."

"No, I am practical. I know that if the people I love can learn to tolerate each other my life will be far more serene."

"Is serenity what you want?" His hand slid along her side.

"If it had been, do you think I would have agreed to be your wife?"

"I thought it was because you could not resist me—
and this."

She gazed up at his smile as his fingers flowed like a
silken web along her body. His gentle, questing kiss
swept aside every thought but of being in his arms.

At a crash and the sound of something shattering,
Priscilla pulled back. "What was that?"

Neville sprinted along the upper gallery, then paused
with a laugh. "I should have guessed."

"Guessed what?" she asked as she edged closer to
him.

He pointed to the lower floor. On it were porcelain
shards. One Chinese vase was pushed back against the
niche and the other in pieces on the floor. "Chester
seems determined to keep everything out of his niche."

"Who is Chester?"

"Chester is a what." He went to the top of the steps
and called, "Here, kitty-kitty-kitty."

"A cat?" She saw a ginger-colored cat not much older
than a kitten coming up the stairs. It was followed by a
gray-striped cat. "How many cats are there here?"

"I have seen at least a dozen different ones." He
grinned at her. "So far. Mayhap I did not mention in my
letter to you that Shadows Fall has always been home to
quite a herd of cats."

She grimaced.

"What is wrong?" he asked.

"Cats make Aunt Cordelia sneeze." This was *not* a
good beginning for their visit.

TWO

Priscilla sat straight up in bed. What was *that?* Groans. It sounded like someone being tortured!

She tried to scramble out of bed and struck the wall. What . . . ? She blinked and stared at the pale light coming in the window. The window was the wrong size and in the wrong place for her home in Stonehall-on-Sea or the house on Bedford Square in London or her aunt's house near Bath. Where was she?

Realization flooded through her, and she sat back on the bed. She was not in Stonehall-on-Sea or London or Bath. She was at Neville's house in Cornwall. Leaning forward, she propped her elbows on her knees and rested her aching forehead on her palms.

How long had she been asleep? Not more than a couple of hours, if she judged by the position of the moon. She had not thought anything could wake her, because she had been sapped by the long, rough journey to Shadows Fall and the effort to capture as many of the cats as possible and shut them in the kitchen. There, they should not bother her aunt.

A groan rumbled through the room. She threw aside the musty bed curtains and listened intently. She heard Leah's soft snores. She saw no motion from Daphne's cot close to the hearth, so her older daughter must be sound asleep.

Could it have been her imagination? No, she knew better than that. Had the talk of smugglers upset her enough to cause a nightmare? Unlikely, for when Lazarus had served in the church in Stonehall-on-Sea, she had been well aware of which men were involved in voyages to the Continent.

Going to the bedroom's window, she opened it. The hushed swish of waves swept into the room. In the distance, she heard what sounded like a horn. It repeated, and she laughed shakily. That must be a sheep seeking its herd. Or could there be seals on the rocks below the cliffs?

Another groan. *That* was not her imagination, and it was neither sheep nor seals. The sound came from outside the house, but where? And what was causing it?

She waited to hear it again, hoping she could pinpoint its location, but like a child counting the seconds in anticipation of a rumble of thunder in the wake of a lightning flash from a distant storm, she waited futilely. Clutching the windowsill, she strained to catch the sound. She sat on the bed when her ears throbbed with her efforts. That throb was swallowed by her headache.

The sound did not come again, and she closed the window as icy air burst in. On the morrow, she would ask Neville if he had heard the noise. He seldom missed anything interesting or troublesome, and he had a way of finding out answers to the most puzzling matters, even a groan in the middle of the night.

Priscilla had no expectation of finding a breakfast parlor within the half-ruined house, so she was not surprised when she was given directions leading to what she guessed had been the house's solar. The ceiling was a masterpiece. Carved wood crisscrossed it. Some pieces jutted down to create an intriguing pattern of light and shadows above the stone floor. Windows, each one divided by diamond-shaped mullions, made up three walls of the room. On the fourth wall was a fireplace large enough that Neville could have stood up inside it and stretched out his arms without touching both sides. A fire crackled there as she walked to a long, rectangular table. At one end, a simple cloth covered objects she guessed were plates of food. A sideboard by the windows was covered with dust.

The room was empty. Her daughters were asleep, and Aunt Cordelia preferred to take breakfast in her private chamber, but she had thought Neville would be here. He seldom kept the hours the *ton* did in Town, which was amazing because he had spent many years in the theater, where the performances often stretched late into the night.

Mrs. Crosby came into the room, smiling gamely. Her apron was spotted with whatever she had been trying to clean, and her sleeves were damp almost to the elbows.

"Sir Neville asked me," the housekeeper said, "to let you know he may be late arriving for breakfast and for you to go ahead without him."

"Where is he?"

"He mentioned yesterday he wanted to check the east tower, which seems to be tilting at a strange angle. I fear it may have to be taken down, leaving the three at the other corners of the house." She glanced around. "Lady Priscilla, there is so much to do here. I doubt anyone has tried living here since King George first went mad."

"Then you have made wondrous strides in making even a part of the house liveable."

Mrs. Crosby smiled, revealing a dimple in her right cheek. "Thank you, my lady. May I bring you some hot chocolate?"

"That would be lovely." Priscilla went to the table as the housekeeper left.

Eggs and warm muffins waited under the cloths across the serving dishes. She glanced up, but saw no sign of any creatures in the rafters. Mayhap they had already been banished. She hoped so.

Selecting scrambled eggs and an apple muffin, Priscilla sat on the chair closest to the hearth. The sun was bright, yet sent feeble heat through the windows. She set her plate on a cleared section of the table. The old oak glistened with recent care.

Footsteps entered the room, and she said, "Mrs. Crosby, you have worked miracles."

"She has, hasn't she?" replied a voice far deeper than the housekeeper's. Strong hands settled on her shoulders.

Priscilla smiled up at Neville. "Your inspection of the east tower must have gone quickly."

"Very, because there appears little hope of salvaging it." He bent down and kissed her cheek. Priscilla caught a whiff of—what?—but he distracted her by kissing her other check. "Kissing you before breakfast is a habit I look forward to developing."

"A good habit?"

He laughed. "In spite of assertions to the contrary, I can assure you that I have a few good habits. I try not to overuse them. Think what that would do to my reputation."

"Indeed." She stroked his cheek, then drew her fingers back when Mrs. Crosby bustled into the room with the chocolate pot and a pair of cups. "You are very discerning, Mrs. Crosby, to guess that Sir Neville was returning just now."

"No foreknowledge on my part." She smiled. "Ennis came into the kitchen as I was leaving to tell me that the inspection of the tower was complete."

"Ennis is a footman," Neville answered before Priscilla could ask the question in her head. "I hired several young people from Trepoole, the last village you passed through on your way here, to assist Mrs. Crosby and Stoddard." Taking the chocolate pot and cups from the housekeeper, he said, "Thank you."

The housekeeper went to tend to her other duties as Neville poured a cup of chocolate for Priscilla. When he set it in front of her, she again caught a smell of foulness, from his navy blue coat.

"Have you been rolling in garbage?" she asked, her nose wrinkling.

"By Jove, Pris, I am sorry." He shrugged off his coat and hung it from one corner of the mantel. "Everything in the tower was damp and disgusting. I doubt if anything in it is salvageable." He smiled. "I trust you will excuse my undress at breakfast."

She knew she should give him some pert answer, but she seemed unable to think of one as she admired how his blue-striped waistcoat accented his lean, rugged torso. Buckskin breeches clung to his lower body, and she knew she should not stare.

Hastily she looked down at her plate as she jabbed at some eggs. Even though she was now betrothed to Neville, she must remember herself. Aunt Cordelia believed the worst of him—and now of Priscilla—and would be watching for any untoward behavior as an excuse to pressure her to discontinue the wedding plans.

"What is wrong, Pris?" Neville asked as he sat across from her.

"I was thinking of my aunt and her dismay."

He chuckled as he poured himself some chocolate. "At my casual state at breakfast? Or at the condition of Shadows Fall?" He leaned one elbow on the table. "Or at me?"

"Why are you asking when you already know the answer?"

His smile faded, and she knew her retort had been too waspish. "What is really wrong, Pris?"

"Did you hear any queer sounds last night?" she asked.

"Sounds?" His eyes narrowed as they did when he was puzzled. "What sort of sounds?"

"Groans."

"Groans? You are jesting, right?"

"No."

He laughed. "Mayhap your aunt—"

"Neville, I am not joking. I heard something last night. A low, rumbling sound. To me, it sounded like a groan, but it could have been something else."

"The wind?"

"No, the wind sounds more like a shriek than a groan."

"The seals on the rocks off the shore?" He set his cup down untouched.

"I considered it might be caused by seals or even by sheep, but it was neither a bark nor a bleat."

"Which direction did it come from?"

She wanted to thank him for believing her when she was not quite sure she believed herself. "I do not know.

By the time I got to the window and realized it was not what I hoped it to be, I did not hear it again to judge where it might be coming from."

He shook his head. "Just a disembodied groan? How about something that goes bump in the night?"

"I told you that I was not hoaxing you. I wanted to warn you in case—"

"In case of what?"

"I don't know. Must you be contrary, Neville, when I am trying to explain what I heard?"

Taking her hand, he gave her a gentle smile. "I am trying to lift you from your dismals. It is not like you, Pris, to be panicked by the sound of the wind."

"I told you. It was not the sound of the wind."

"Then what do you suggest it was? A ghost, mayhap?"

"I do not believe in ghosts," she said. "I do believe, however, that I heard something unusual. I wanted to alert you in case you hear it, too."

He nodded. "Thank you for the warning, and I promise you I will not disturb you in the middle of the night if I hear ghostly groans so you may say you told me so."

"Neville, save your sarcasm for someone else."

"Forgive me, Pris." He squeezed her hand. "It seems my efforts to cheer you up are failing completely."

"I want you to believe me."

"Of course, I believe you. I am unsure what else to say, and it seems you are eager for answers."

"I am curious what the sound was."

"That is no surprise. You are a curious woman."

Priscilla smiled, pleased his teasing was finally vanquishing her disquiet. "How do you mean that?"

"Do not read meaning into my words that I have not intended."

"I suspect you always mean more than you say."

"Quite true. You are a woman with a strong curiosity that must be appeased, and you are a woman unlike any other I have ever met." He lifted her hand to his lips. "Quite the curiosity in yourself."

"Neville—"

A shriek resounded through the house. Something crashed. Something large, for the floor shook beneath Priscilla's feet. The windows rattled, and debris dropped from the ceiling.

Neville grabbed her arm and tugged her under the table. Her right knee banged hard on the floor. She bit back her moan when a thick board fell from the ceiling, striking her chair and breaking both into pieces. Something hit the table right over their heads. The table shivered and china shattered, raining down around them, but the table did not collapse.

Then it was silent. Dust swirled through the air.

"Are you hurt, Pris?" Neville asked.

"Not bad. Thanks to you. Are you all right?"

"Almost."

"What? What is wrong?"

He slipped his arm around her and turned her up against him. "Having you so far away in this bower is wrong."

His hands settled on her upper arms. He slid them up to cup her face. The kiss he pressed onto her lips was hotter than the fire snapping on the hearth. She drew back at shouts from beyond the room.

"Not yet," he whispered. When he captured her lips again, she ran her fingers up his back and softened against him. She was grateful he was unharmed.

An ear-splitting shriek came from nearby, and Priscilla pulled herself out of Neville's arms again.

"Oh, they must be dead!" came a moan from the doorway.

"Not yet," Neville said as he pushed aside the cloth that had covered the dishes. Plaster dust fell about them in a thick, gray cloud. Crawling out from under the table, he stretched back his arm to help Priscilla clamber out from beneath it. He brought her to her feet, and as she sneezed, he smiled at his ashen-faced butler. "Stoddard, you ought to know that a mere earthquake is not enough to put an end to the Hathaway line."

Color flooded back into Stoddard's face, which became composed as he replied, "It was no earthquake, Sir Neville. The east tower has tumbled down."

"The east tower?" Priscilla pressed her hand over her rapidly beating heart. She sneezed again and again and nodded her thanks when Neville gave her his handkerchief.

"How is that possible?" Neville lifted his coat off the mantel and shook dust from it. Pulling it on, he said, "The tower seemed stable when Ennis and I checked it less than an hour ago."

Stoddard shook his head. "I cannot say, sir. I know nothing about construction."

"I was not looking for an answer, just thinking out loud." Neville frowned. "Was anyone in or near the tower?"

"I am unsure."

"Then we need to find out." He glanced at Priscilla. "Excuse me, Pris, while I make sure everyone is safe."

"Of course," she replied. "I will go and see how Daphne and Leah and Aunt Cordelia fare." She took a single step, then grimaced as pain flashed from the knee she had struck on the floor.

"Pris?" His arm was around her waist as he leaned her

against him so she did not have to put weight on her right leg.

"I will be all right." She smiled. "Just a bruise, Neville, and it is far less than I would have suffered if you had not acted quickly." Her smile wavered when she looked at the crushed chair. "Go, and make sure the rest of your household is unharmed."

He caressed her cheek and nodded. Motioning to Stoddard to come with him, Neville hurried out of the room.

Priscilla limped as she climbed the steps, but the pain was already working its way out by the time she reached the door of the room she shared with her daughters. It opened as she put out her hand to the knob.

"Mama!" cried Daphne, flinging her arms around Priscilla.

"Take care." Lifting her daughter's arms away, she smiled as pieces of plaster clattered to the floor. She must look a sight covered with the gray dust. "Don't be frightened. Some old walls collapsed."

Leah was standing on her cot and peering out the window. "Mama, it was a whole tower!"

"You can see it from here?" Priscilla rushed to the window, paying no attention to the twinge in her knee.

She could not even gasp when she stared at the stone spread between the east corner of the house and the stables. Some pieces were larger than her carriage. One stone had rolled to a stop, tilting against another wall, as if it had been tossed there by a giant child. Another had broken off a tree whose branches had been driven through a barn roof.

"We felt the first rumble," Leah said, bouncing from her cot to the bed. "We looked out in time to see it topple. It went straight over." Raising one hand, she brought it down against the other in a sharp clap. "Just like that. Boom!"

"Was anyone hurt?" asked Daphne.

Priscilla put her arm around her older daughter, who edged closer to her. "Neville has gone to check, but it is unlikely. No one was in the tower when Neville was in there earlier this morning."

"He was in there this morning?" Leah dropped to sit on the bed. "Mama, imagine if the tower had fallen over then."

"I would prefer not to." Brushing her hands against her dress, she frowned as more plaster fell to the floor. "I should change before your aunt sees me. I am surprised she has not checked on you already."

"Do you want me to look in on her, Mama?" Daphne asked.

"Please, but give me time to repair the damage done to me before you allow her in here."

"*Allow* her? Mama, Aunt Cordelia is unstoppable."

Priscilla motioned for Leah to unhook her. "Do your best, Daphne. It will be good practice for—"

"For dealing with old toughs during the Season," Daphne finished with a grimace.

Listening to her younger daughter chattering about what she had seen through the window, Priscilla changed into a cream-colored morning gown. She drew on her high-lows, because she wanted to see the fallen tower more closely. When Leah pleaded to go along, Priscilla promised to take her daughters to see the rubble after they finished their breakfast.

Daphne was walking toward the bedroom when Priscilla came out into the hallway, holding her bonnet and her cloak draped over one arm. Nodding when Daphne told her that Aunt Cordelia was still asleep, apparently not being awakened by the tower's fall, Priscilla repeated her request that Daphne and Leah have breakfast while waiting for Priscilla to return for them.

"I will have Mrs. Crosby send breakfast to you," Priscilla said, tying her straw bonnet's white ribbons beneath her chin. "It will be a long time before breakfast can be served in the solar again."

"I guessed that by the dust on you, Mama."

"Keep Leah from following me."

"Another challenge to teach me something for the Season, I assume."

Laughing at her daughter's grim tone, Priscilla went down the steps at a pace that would have earned her children a scolding. A lanky footman was standing at the base of the lower staircase. He bowed his head, his blond hair falling forward into his eyes. Gray dust covered his hair and had dimmed any shine on his boots.

"Are you Ennis?" she asked as she tossed her cloak over her shoulders.

"Yes, my lady." His words were laced with a strong Cornish accent. He ran his fingers through his hair and grimaced when thick dust cascaded to the floor.

"I am very glad to see you alive."

"I am very glad to be alive." His eyes widened. "Mayhap I should have not spoken so."

"You would be wise to err on the side of forthrightness when you serve Sir Neville."

Ennis grinned, looking no older than Isaac. She had to be glad her son was not at Shadows Fall. By this time, he would have been crawling over the debris.

"Sir Neville told me to bring you out to what remains of the east tower," Ennis said. "He was certain you would wish to see it for yourself."

"He was right." As she went with Ennis along a hallway leading toward the back of the house, she tried to ignore the stench. This corridor smelled like a half-forgotten privy. A great deal of work would be required to clean it, and she wondered if it might be wiser to empty out the house and pull the whole thing down.

"The smell improves in a few more feet," Ennis said.

"Do you know what is causing it?"

He nodded. "Most likely the ghosts are trying to get the living to leave them alone again."

"Ghosts?"

"Didn't you know Shadows Fall is haunted?"

"By whom?"

"Several ghosts. One is said to be a Spaniard who died on the rocks below when one of the last surviving ships of the Armada sank. Then there is the spirit of Sir Ambrose. He lived here during the Civil War." He drew his finger across his throat. "And he chose the wrong side."

"Any others?"

"One ghost seen by wreckers." He laughed. "They will not see him any longer because he was in the east tower."

"There are wreckers here?"

He did not meet her eyes as he mumbled something that sounded like, "Not any longer."

Priscilla did not believe him. Cornwall was far from London, and she would not be astonished to discover if the local constable turned a blind eye to such activities. Even along Sussex's shore, there were rumors of shipwrecks that had not been accidents. Only rumors, because everyone knew the danger of speaking specific names and places. The wreckers were reputed to fear no one, not even the law, and would silence anyone who betrayed them.

Her late husband, Lazarus, might have known more

than most about them, because he had been called from his church often enough to speak a blessing over a body washed ashore. On that subject, unlike any others, he was reticent. Priscilla's curiosity had gained her nothing, and she had understood why when a man was found hanged near the shore. It had been whispered in Stonehall-on-Sea he was a wrecker who had prattled like a young miss while foxed in a local tavern. He had been silenced as a warning to others.

As they came out of the house, the chill wind from the sea toyed with Priscilla's cloak. She took a deep breath of fresh air. She choked on it when she looked at the damage in front of her. The destruction was even more astounding when she stood beside the huge chunks of stone and could see how they had tumbled like a stack of blocks.

"Walk here," Ennis said, gesturing to his right. "It is the only way not clogged with stone. Take care, my lady. Some pieces may not be completely settled."

Weaving through a madman's re-creation of a standing stone circle, she followed Ennis toward what had been the base of the tower. She looked up at the house. Where the tower had stood, doors opened into the sky. Several had drapes hung in them, probably in an effort to keep drafts from seeping through the rickety tower. Now that fabric flapped in the cold breeze.

"Over here," came Neville's shout. "Watch out for the glass in the grass. A few of the windows were still intact."

Priscilla picked her way through the grass. The sun had already melted away any hints of frost, so she was able to see where the shards had scattered. As soon as she reached where he was kneeling, examining a stone, she asked, "Can you tell what happened?"

Neville stood and wiped dirt from his hands. On his

forehead, blood was drying. He must have been struck by something in the solar. "The earth gave way beneath one corner of the tower." Taking her hand, he led her around the chunk of stone while Ennis walked back toward the house. "Right here."

What was left of the round walls tilted into a depression. Looking down into the foundation, she saw water pooled at one side. "It appears this tower has been on its way down for a while."

"So it would seem, but the floors were not too slanted when Ennis and I examined it. Something must have shifted suddenly."

"An earthquake?"

"Possible, but I would have thought the sea would show the aftereffects, and it is as calm as I have ever seen it." He offered his arm. When she had put her hand on it, he walked toward a rise near the cliff's edge. "As you can see, Pris, there have been continual shifts in the land over eons."

She stared at the stone carved by the sea and the wind. One outcropping reminded her of a chessboard's bishop. What appeared to be caves were cut into the cliffs, most of them so shallow she could reach the back in a few steps. Far to the north, she saw an outcropping topped by a large plateau.

"Does anyone live there?" she asked.

"Not any longer. See the ruined walls?" He pointed to thin, dark lines. "If we could step back in time, we might see Camelot rise from the ruins at Tintagel."

"Camelot? King Arthur?"

"According to the monk Geoffrey of Monmouth, Arthur was conceived by magic at Tintagel. He may have even grown up there."

"Geoffrey or Arthur?"

He laughed. "Pris, must you always be practical? I had thought the idea of being able to see where the Knights of the Round Table might have gathered would appeal to you. I had even considered asking if you and Daphne and Leah would like to visit the site and the village of Trevena beside it."

"Most days, such a site would be of great interest to me."

"But right now you are thinking only of why the tower collapsed."

"Yes." Turning her back on distant Tintagel, she appraised the scattered stone. "If the earth slipped from beneath one tower, what assurance is there that it will not happen to the others?"

"None." He took her hand and helped her around a large stone that had been discolored on one side by salt blown off the sea. On another side, it was painted a bleak green. "Mayhap this is not such a loss. Some of my ancestors had no taste."

"I see no walls painted red."

"Exactly." He leaned against a darkened stone that was almost as tall as he was. "I thought bright colors would herald a new beginning at Shadows Fall."

"You might have asked me."

Tapping her nose, he said, "You are not the chatelaine yet, Pris. Besides, I believe you like the color."

"I suspect I shall accustom myself to it as I have about so many other aspects of life with you."

He put his arms around her waist. "You need not make it sound like such a dreary task."

"Neville," she said, easing out of his arms although she wanted to remain within them, "there are questions I must ask you."

"They can wait." He drew her back to him.

"Will you stop?" She put her hands on his chest to push him away.

He did not let her step back this time. "Not likely, for I know you would be most displeased with me, Pris, if I let you go and never held you close to me again." He pressed his lips to her neck.

Quivers surged through her as her fingers clutched onto his sleeves. Bother! Why was he always right when it came to matters of love? As his mouth coursed along her skin and he left tender nibbles along her jaw, she longed to toss propriety aside. His tongue teased her ear, and she moaned with the desire to yield to him and this pleasure.

He found her lips, and she welcomed his eager kiss. He might be a prime rogue, the very worst match for a parson's widow, but she could not imagine her life without him—and his kisses.

At that thought, she stiffened.

He raised his mouth. "Don't tell me something is wrong, Pris, when I am holding you."

"I must." Reaching past him, she ran her fingers along the stone. Black smudged on them. She held her fingers to her nose. "This smells like gunpowder."

"Gunpowder?" His face hardened as he grabbed her hand and held it close to his face. He sniffed. "It does. There must have been some stored in the tower."

"Who knew you and Ennis were going to be in the tower this morning?"

His face hardened. "Stoddard. My valet. Anyone who saw us going out there, but, Pris, who would have known the tower was going to crash to the ground when it did?"

"If that gunpowder was not stored there, it could be left from an explosion set off to bring the tower down."

He shook his head. "You saw the hollow where the

tower collapsed. The ground gave way beneath the tower."

"You may be right, but hear me out."

"All right."

"Neville, did someone suggest you go there this morning rather than another time?"

"No."

"Did Ennis seem unduly uneasy?"

"No. He offered to go with me, and he seemed curious because, as he told me, nobody from the village dared to go inside. Not even on a wager. He wanted to see what was in the tower."

"Probably he was hoping to find the ghost seen by wreckers." She quickly explained what Ennis had told her.

"Any ghosts within have been quite rudely evicted." He started to chuckle, then grew serious when she did not laugh along with him.

"Was Ennis with you all the time?"

He shook his head. "Not all the time. Pris, this speculation is silly. Nobody could have known the tower would fall as it did. Even if someone wished me harm, making it tumble this morning would be quite an accomplishment."

"It would be . . . unless someone used gunpowder. What if the groans I heard last night were from men rigging an explosion?"

"You said you had no idea which direction the sound came from."

"True." She brushed his forehead, close to the wound that still oozed blood. "But it is also true, that, whether I am seeing trouble where there is none or whether my suspicions are correct, we must consider the fact that someone may want you dead."

THREE

Neville nodded his thanks to Riley when his valet held out a clean coat. Drawing it on, he frowned.

"Do you wish another, sir?" asked the valet.

"Another?"

"Coat."

"This one is fine." Although he knew Riley wished he took more interest in clothing, Neville did not have time to indulge his valet.

What if Priscilla was right? She could not be—the very idea that someone wanted to kill him was ludicrous. He had no enemies in Cornwall. In other parts of England, he could not have said that. This was his first visit to Shadows Fall.

He would not be at the estate now if he had a hint of intelligence. When the idea had come into his head that this might make an excellent home for him and Priscilla after their wedding, it had seemed so simple. Priscilla enjoyed Town, but she preferred the country. So often in the years he had known her, she had spoken of her love for living beside the ocean, as she did in Stonehall-on-Sea. Her home there, Mermaid Cottage, was one she had shared with her late husband. He had imagined Shadows Fall as the perfect place to make a home for Priscilla and himself.

Then he had arrived and discovered the house was far from what he had expected. That the house reeked and was barely habitable were only two of its faults. Whoever had last lived in this house had had a unique idea of good taste. He hoped the servants would recall their promise not to mention anything to Priscilla or her family about the murals he had spent the past fortnight painting over. Those murals would have made a courtesan blush, and Priscilla would not have wanted her daughters to view the indiscreet paintings.

He wiggled his fingers. He had not painted since his early days in the theater when he had been assigned the job of making scenery.

As if privy to Neville's thoughts, Riley said, "Garland asked me to let you know, sir, that more paint has been prepared."

"More red?"

Riley smiled faintly. "I am not certain of the shade, but I can find out."

"No need. I am done painting. I shall leave the job in far more capable hands."

"Yes, sir." Riley's smile widened. The valet could not hide that he wished Neville would, more often, act as Riley believed a member of the Polite World should.

Neville walked out of the bedchamber, which was even more cramped than the room Priscilla and her daughters had used last night. Stepping around a maid sweeping debris that must have fallen at the same time the tower did, he continued along the hallway. He hoped Stoddard had been able to hire more servants from the nearby village. Trepoole had many young people looking for work, but he was uncertain if they wanted honest work.

As he came around a corner, he stepped aside to

avoid Mrs. Crosby. The housekeeper was walking at a rapid pace, a determined expression on her face.

She drew herself up. "Forgive me, sir."

"No need for an apology."

"The house, save for the solar, is almost back to rights." Her nose wrinkled. "Or as right as it was before the tower toppled. Stoddard has some of the lads cleaning out another room suitable for dining."

"I trust he is keeping everyone out of the solar. I doubt the ceiling is very stable."

"He has warned the staff."

"And I shall warn Lady Priscilla's younger daughter." He chuckled. "Leah has inherited her curiosity from her mother."

"We will watch she does not go in there, sir."

"Thank you." He edged around her. "Do you know where Lady Priscilla is?"

Mrs. Crosby nodded so vehemently her cap almost bounced off her head. "She asked me to ask you to join her in the parlor."

"Parlor? Which room have you designated the parlor, Mrs. Crosby?"

"The sitting room overlooking the sea across the stairs from the solar."

Neville hid his amusement at her amazed response. Like the other servants he had inherited along with his title, Mrs. Crosby seemed to consider his questions, even the most mundane, baffling. He had never met the man who had bequeathed him the family's title and assets, but that distant relative must have fit into the Hathaway family of eccentrics.

And being odd was no cause for anyone to murder him. Priscilla, most uncharacteristically, was overreacting to an accident. Even as he told himself that, a small voice, with absolute honesty, reminded him that becoming hysterical was something he had never seen her do.

As he entered the room that could be called small only in a house of this size, for it was wider and deeper than his house on Berkeley Square, he saw Priscilla reaching for a book on shelves between a pair of windows. She did not see him, so he had a rare chance to admire her without her noticing. Her golden hair surrounded a face that belied her age—and the fact that she was the mother of a young woman about to be fired off on her first Season. Her slender figure was accented perfectly by her simple gown, which only hinted at the curves he had felt against him when he drew her into his arms.

He had known her since she was not much older than Daphne, for her husband had been his best friend. Lazarus had treated his wife with a respect and kindness that allowed her to bloom into the wondrous woman she had become. Then Lazarus had died suddenly almost two years ago, and Neville had been bereft. Not only for the loss of his friend, but for Priscilla's absence in his life. As soon as she had completed her mourning, he had sought her out, wondering if she had missed him as well. He had intended to rebuild their friendship, never owning to himself that he had hoped for more than friendship. He could not have done so because he had not known the truth himself until he began to imagine a future he had never wanted before. A future with a wife and a family and the life he had once derided as filled with unending ennui.

"Have you come to your senses?" asked Priscilla.

He had not noticed her looking in his direction, for he had been too caught up in his thoughts. Vexed at himself, he retorted, "Have you?"

Her eyes widened in dismay, and he wanted to take back the barbed question. By Jove! It was not his intention to distress her more.

"Yes," she answered stiffly. "I have come to my senses as I did when I did not discount the evidence right in front of my eyes because it was inconvenient."

Crossing the room, weaving a path between the trio of settees and the half-dozen tables brought into the room for safekeeping while he painted, Neville said, "I have considered this matter, and I cannot imagine who in Cornwall would wish me such a fate."

"Did you consider that Cornwall might prove to be an advantageous venue for crime? Everyone knows smugglers thrive here. What better place than to exact a little revenge and murder?"

"Pris, your mind is fixed on evildoings today."

She sat on the window seat, then held out her hand to him. "Do you believe my concerns for you have muddied my thinking?"

He took her hand. It was trembling as he sat beside her. He wanted it to tremble, not with fear, but with anticipation of his touch. Pressing her fingers to his lips, he savored her sweet skin. He raised his head to see her eyes glowing with delight.

Although he ached to kiss her, he said, "No, Pris. You are the most clear-thinking woman I know. Nay, make that the most clear-thinking *person* I know. Given what you believe to be fact, I can understand why you have come to certain conclusions."

"But you believe I am wrong."

"Yes."

"Why do you think so when you have trusted my judgment before?"

"Because . . ." He frowned.

"You can be honest with me, Neville."

He brushed her cheek with a crooked finger. "I always try to be, sweetheart. That is why I am faltering on my answer."

"Because you have none?"

"Yes."

She put her hand on his chest, and he wondered if his heart had metamorphosed into a runaway horse. It seemed ready to leap right through his skin to find hers. Her soft voice was a splendid song, so splendid he had to force himself to focus on her words.

"Neville, I may be right or I may be wrong. Either way, it behooves us to consider all possibilities, as we have done in the past."

"In the past? Pris, your mind dwells too much on murder and mayhem."

"A trait I must have acquired from spending time with you."

He laughed. Dash it! Getting into a brangle with her was futile. She was too quick with her answers, and she knew him too well.

Slipping his arm around her, he said, "I cannot argue with that, but, Pris, I need more proof than stains from gunpowder that might be as old as Guy Fawkes himself."

"I would rather you do not find it."

"As do I." He tipped her chin toward him. "Pris, have I told you how much I missed you?"

"Yes."

"Have I *showed* you how much I missed you?"

A beguiling smile curved along her lips. "Not enough, Neville."

"Then let me rectify that oversight."

Her eyes closed as he bent toward her mouth. They popped open as his name was called from the hallway.

Putting his finger against her lips, he said, "Don't forget you owe me a kiss, sweetheart."

"I will not, but I may need you to remind me."

"Mayhap I should remind you now."

"Mayhap you should." She leaned toward him, and he was unable to resist the mesmerizing temptation of her lips.

"Am I interrupting?" asked someone behind him.

Neville turned to see a footman coming into the room. The red-haired lad was a stranger, so Neville guessed he was another lad hired by Stoddard. An impudent grin creased the footman's face, but it vanished as the butler appeared in the doorway.

"Forgive Harwood," Stoddard said with a stern glance at the lad. "He needs to learn to enter a room without announcing himself."

Neville stood and walked toward the two men. "I trust he will learn quickly."

"Yes, sir," the lad replied at the same time as Stoddard, earning him another glare from the butler.

"Go ahead," Stoddard added. "Do what I sent you to do."

The lad inched forward and held out a folded sheet. "Sir Neville, sir, this was delivered for you, sir."

"Thank you." Neville took the page. "Is there anyone waiting for a reply?"

"No, Sir Neville, sir, there is no one waiting, sir."

Stoddard herded the new footman into the hallway, and Neville heard a hushed laugh behind him. Looking back, he saw Priscilla holding her hand over her mouth.

"Go ahead," he said. "Say it."

"Say what, Sir Neville, sir?" She crossed the room. "You completely intimidated that poor lad with a handful of words."

"Some people find me intimidating, Pris."

Her smile vanished. "And that is why I am concerned."

"Dash it, Pris! That was not what I meant. A new footman stumbling over his words is not sufficient reason to reinforce your belief that I escaped death at an enemy's hands."

"I need nothing to strengthen my belief." Priscilla wanted to take Neville by the arms and shake some sense into him. It was so unlike him to denounce the facts without further investigation. "Mayhap you should read what has been delivered to you."

He frowned, and she knew her tone had been as honed as his when he entered the room. Even though he was disavowing any connection between the tower falling and his safety, he was unsettled.

"Mayhap I should." He opened the page and scanned it. "I fear our betrothal party has been trumped by another invitation."

"An invitation?"

"Of a sort." He held it out. "Do you think Daphne and Leah would be interested? I know Isaac would be, but he will have to accept the invitation on his next holiday."

Curious, Priscilla took the slip of paper. It took her a moment to decipher handwriting that would have earned her son a reprimand from his tutor.

My dear Sir Neville,

    I have heard that you have taken up residence in Shadows Fall. My assistant and I would welcome a visit at your earliest convenience, so we may show you the work we wish to do on your property. Lord Beddlemere suggested that you would be willing to let us work on your land as well as his, and I look forward to speaking with you to discover if he is correct.

You are invited to call on any clear day from sunrise to sunset.

I am your humble servant.

Williston Dyson

"Who is Williston Dyson?" she asked.

"From what I heard in Trepoole, Professor Dyson studies history. Ancient history." Taking the paper, he folded it. "He has been doing some digging close to the shore. I believe he is hoping to uncover ruins from when the Romans settled this area."

"How interesting!"

"Yes." He smiled. "Just the thing to get your mind off dreary matters."

"If you think a few old trinkets will distract me from my worries, you are mistaken."

"Not a few old trinkets." He tossed the page on a table and, sweeping his arm around her, pulled her close to him. "I had rather hoped that *this* would."

When his mouth slanted across hers, she had to own he had chosen the very thing that could halt her alarmed thoughts for a few, joyous minutes.

The climb down to where Professor Dyson was digging in search of artifacts was steep enough to daunt even Priscilla, who often took, in Neville's opinion, too many risks. Today she was being wise, watching out for herself and her daughters. While the sea breeze buffeted them, she clasped Neville's hand as they traversed the edge of the cliffs. Unlike the chalk ones near Stonehall-on-Sea, these cliffs were gray rock. Sharp edges and outcroppings even beyond where the waves broke suggested only a fool or a very savvy navigator would try to bring a boat to shore here.

He gazed out over the sea. Would he ever grow tired of admiring the water that changed with each motion of the sun and the vagaries of the weather? He should have come to Shadows Fall before, but there always had been something to prevent him from making the long journey.

When Priscilla grasped his arm with her other hand, he smiled. *She* was the reason he had been diverted for the past year, and she was a most pleasant disturbance to what had been a well-ordered life enjoying the camaraderie of his friends and a comfortable existence on Berkeley Square.

Priscilla glanced to her right toward the strand. "Is that another cave?"

"There are many along this stretch of the shore."

"For pirates?" asked Leah, leaning on one of the boulders along the cliff's edge.

Drawing her back, Neville said, "That is possible. Cornwall has a long history, both legal and less than legal, with the sea."

"Is that why the Hathaways lived here?"

"Leah!" chided Priscilla.

"Don't scold her for a legitimate question." Neville laughed when Priscilla grimaced at his choice of words. "I have little knowledge of my ancestors' activities, so I am hoping to learn more. I am sure it will be interesting."

Leah clapped her hands in delight, then reached for her bonnet, which had soared off her head. Daphne caught it and handed the bonnet to her younger sister. They giggled as they skirted another large boulder.

They slowed only when Priscilla called after them to take care.

Priscilla started to follow, then paused by the boulder. With a laugh, Neville picked her up by the waist and swung her over it.

When he set her down on the ground, she gasped, "Will you please warn me before you do something like that again?"

"Then you would not have this pretty flush." He climbed atop it and jumped down beside her. His boot skidded on the ground, and his arms windmilled.

She pushed him back against the rock. He put his arms around her before she could slip from the barely visible path.

"You saved my life," he said with another chuckle.

"Then you are in my debt."

"True. What is your price for saving a life, Pris? Can I hope it is a kiss or two?" He gave her a rakish leer. "Or a hundred?"

"All I want you to do is hold on to that life and not throw it away carelessly."

His brows lowered. "I had no intentions of doing so."

"Good." Stepping back, she held out her hand. "We must be getting close to where Professor Dyson is digging."

He nodded. They had almost reached the southern border of the lands belonging to Shadows Fall. The upward slope marked the boundary between Shadows Fall and Lord Beddlemere's property. He had not had a chance to meet the neighboring marquess, but he had heard much of the man in Trepoole. Little of what he had heard was complimentary because Beddlemere had evicted his tenants and now used his lands solely for his sheep. The mines had been closed even though there was still ore within them.

Yet Beddlemere was allowing Professor Dyson to dig up his fields. Mayhap the man simply had no interest in administering and collecting rents. Neville had learned not to listen to *on dits*, but to form his own opinions based on what he had discovered firsthand. When he had the opportunity to meet Beddlemere, he would find out how much was true and how much was distorted by gossip.

Neville continued to hold Priscilla's hand as the slope eased. Drawing it to his arm, he smiled. Her cheeks were ruddy from the wind, and soft, golden curls had escaped from her chignon to flutter about her face. Anticipation glowed in her eyes. For the professor's work, he wondered, or for a more intimate caress?

His other sleeve was grasped, and he looked to his left to see Leah grinning up at him. Dash it! He had to take care not to get so caught up in the longing for pleasure that he ignored what was happening around him. He had honed his observation skills for many years; he had not thought a woman's captivating smile would vanquish them.

"You should see what Professor Dyson has!" cried Leah.

"We shall," Priscilla said as she held her other hand out to her younger daughter. When Leah took it and continued to grin at Neville, Priscilla let happiness enfold her. Their family had been shattered when Lazarus died. With Neville's help, they were rediscovering joy.

Leah chattered like a bird as they went toward where the earth had been overturned except for a mound in the center of the field. Priscilla had not guessed the excavation covered such a large area. The ground was scarred in a great square from the stone wall to the cliffs several hundred yards away.

"Interesting," Neville said under his breath.

"What is interesting?" she asked.

"I had thought Professor Dyson wished to speak to me about permission to dig up Shadows Fall's lands, but he already is. The far wall marks the boundaries of the estate."

"Certainly you do not intend to halt his work."

"No, but to be asked first would have been considerate."

She laughed. "And when did you ever ask first when you wanted something, Neville? Did you consider you might be having to swallow a dose of your own medicine?"

"I should know better than to grumble to you. You know me too well."

Priscilla almost replied that she knew far too little about him, but asking questions about Neville's past were sure to get her unsatisfactory answers or none at all. He was not ashamed of it, but he preferred to focus on the present and the future.

Two men were working near each other. As Priscilla followed her daughter over the bench stile at the stone wall, she saw stacks of stone had been freed from the ground. They outlined what appeared to be rooms. She reached out to touch a stone that had been buried for more than a millennium. Which emperor had ruled Rome when these buildings were in use?

"It is amazing," Daphne murmured as she came to stand beside them. "I never would have guessed such things were waiting right under the grass."

"Watch where you are stepping!" The order was shouted as a short man with graying hair came toward them. His black coat flapped after him, and a quizzing glass bounced against his dirty waistcoat. Pausing, he lifted the glass and peered through it. "I am Professor Dyson. You are Lady Priscilla, I presume from your daughters' description."

Wondering what else Leah and Daphne might have told him, she said, "Yes, and this is Sir Neville Hathaway."

"Hathaway?" He turned the quizzing glass toward Neville, then dropped it. "Welcome." Turning, he picked up something and shoved it into Neville's arms. "This is an example of what we might find on your estate."

"You are already on my estate."

"Really? I had no idea." The professor shrugged. "Then see what we have found on *your* estate."

Taking more care than Professor Dyson had with the large ceramic pot, Neville tilted it so Priscilla could admire it as well. It had been carved with a scene of stags racing through a wood. A man with a spear was taking aim at one. Another was dead at his feet. Bits of red paint clung to the pot.

"Allow me," said a dark-haired man who held out his hands. Gently he took the pot from Neville and smiled. His brown eyes slitted when he glowered at Professor Dyson, who was ushering Neville toward the edge of the dug-up area and pointing toward Shadows Fall. Daphne and Leah were following the men, eager not to miss a tidbit of information. "Lady Priscilla, I am Oscar Randall, the professor's assistant."

"That is a marvelous pot, Mr. Randall." Priscilla was glad when he looked back at her, a smile returning to his visage.

"Marvelous is the correct word." He ran his fingers

over one deer. "This was created by a skilled artisan." Wrapping the pot in layers of linen, he placed it in a box. "Would you like a tour of the temple and the village?"

"This was a village?"

"Yes. I . . . that is, we believe there was at that time a section of land that has since fallen into the sea. We have barely begun to explore the area nearest to the cliffs." He gestured toward the center of where they had been digging. "Right now, we are exploring the area around the temple."

"Indeed. Tell me more."

"I believe it was Pluto's sanctuary. But the professor disagrees, for he feels it was sacred to Juno. We have yet to find the clues to prove one of us wrong."

"There is quite a difference, Mr. Randall, between those two deities. Pluto was the god of the underworld, and the goddess Juno was concerned with more feminine matters of marriage and family."

He smiled with almost boyish glee, although he was older than she was. "Lady Priscilla, I am very pleased with your knowledge of the pantheon of gods. Does Sir Neville share your familiarity with Roman mythology?"

"I am not sure. It is not a subject we have discussed."

"Oh." He somehow conveyed in that single word his belief that no relationship was complete without such enlightened conversations.

"But you will find Sir Neville eager to learn." She did not let her smile slip as she asked, "Did you see anyone near the east tower of Shadows Fall this morning?"

"East tower?" He shaded his hands and looked toward the house. "It is gone! What happened to it?"

"It fell over. You did not hear anything or see anything or anyone out of the ordinary?"

He shook his head. "We arrived at the site only in the

past hour, my lady. We were meeting with Lord Beddle-mere at his house during the forenoon. I am sorry, my lady, but I cannot help you. I trust no one was hurt."

"No one, thank goodness."

"If you would prefer to look around later—"

"My curiosity about what happened to the tower is matched by my curiosity about this lost settlement."

He smiled, pleased at her interest in the work he was doing and gestured toward the cliffs. "We believe most of the village was lost in a landslide there. Much of what we have uncovered appears to be a complex of temple buildings. Most of the statuary has been removed or broken, which is the root of the disagreement between the professor and myself. We hope to uncover some statues that were left behind and undamaged, so we might have the proof we need."

"You have searched most of it." She looked at the field, which had been dug up except for the mound.

"The temple complex must have been almost twice as big as present-day Trepoole," Mr. Randall said. "The rest of this ancient village would have dwarfed it. It is our belief—one we both share—that this site is many times bigger than the one near the ruins of Tintagel Castle."

"You have found much already, but I am curious as to why you have not dug into that mound."

"We have." He motioned toward it, then matched her steps as they walked between the knee-high rows of stacked stones.

He led her to where an entrance had been cut into the side of the mound. Not by the professor and his assistant, but possibly by the ancient Romans. The lintel was carved, but its pattern had been almost obliterated by time.

When he ducked under the lintel to go in, she followed. It was not dark inside as she had expected, and she looked up to see that a large chunk of the top had been cut away, allowing the sunlight to enter.

"Isn't it magnificent?" Mr. Randall asked.

Priscilla gasped as she stared at the temple, which even in the dappled shadows she could see was incredibly well preserved. It was circular, about ten yards in diameter. No decoration was visible, for the surfaces were encrusted with dirt.

The peristyle had collapsed into a pile of pillars, but the temple walls remained upright. She wondered if the roof was steady. Dozens of other pillars leaned against one another, like a disjointed skeleton. She saw an atlantes, a male figure which would have supported a roof, and several caryatids, their female counterparts. The feminine figures, which had been carved into the columns, were so encrusted it was impossible to tell if they were identical or different.

"Look here," Mr. Randall said. "The front of the temple has hints of murals." He ran his fingers along faces sculpted centuries before.

Her heart skipped a beat when she realized the main mural was intact. The scene seemed to be of a bacchanalian feast. The colors were a phantom of their past splendor. "This is extraordinary."

"You must see inside."

"Is it safe?"

"It seems to be."

Priscilla was uncertain if that was enough assurance, but she could not resist the opportunity to peek into the temple. Standing outside, but craning her neck so she could see within, she stared at what must have been the altar. Sunlight brightened a human face carved of stone. She looked into the eyes, which, if she had been standing in the middle of the stone floor, would have been well above hers. This must be Juno, the patron of the doomed temple. Or Pluto. Or mayhap another god or goddess. For centuries, the stone image had stood guard over the forgotten altar.

She understood Mr. Randall's excitement. Even the floor was beautiful, although the tiles had been ruptured when the ground shifted through the centuries.

"May I?" she asked, pointing to a loose tile.

"Of course." She bent and picked up the broken tile. As she held it up, a brilliant orange burst to life in the sunshine. Her fingers trembled with excitement as she set the tile back. "It is hard to believe that this place was lost."

"Not really lost. We have found evidence that the ancient Celts may have used this place for worship. There are many places in Cornwall the druid priests considered sacred." His nose wrinkled with the disgust that filled his voice as he added, "Not that we are interested in the sites where they practiced human sacrifice." He rubbed his hands together. "Do you think Sir Neville will allow us to continue to work on his lands?" Dismay lengthened his face. "I hope that we have not angered him. I had assumed Professor Dyson knew the limits of where he had permission to dig. Is Sir Neville furious?"

"I have seen no sign of that."

"Then do you think it is possible he will give permission for us to continue our work on his property?"

"I cannot speak for him," Priscilla said, although, after seeing Neville's fascination with the pot, she had no doubts he would give his blessing to this project, "but all you need to do is show him this."

"Show me what?" asked Neville as he ducked beneath the stone lintel. He whistled, but the sound was smothered by the earth of the mound. "You said the best remained hidden, Professor. I had no idea you meant something like this."

Professor Dyson grinned as if he had invented the whole of this for their enjoyment. "It is amazing, is it not?"

Priscilla caught Leah's arm before her daughter could rush into the temple. "The roof may not be secure, so you must not go inside until it has been stabilized."

"May we look around the rest of the mound?" Leah asked.

"Yes, but don't climb under or on anything. With all the work being done in the field beyond this mound, the ground may have been disturbed enough to make this less sturdy than it appears."

"You fret too much, Mama."

"Because she has cause to." Neville tapped Leah's nose and chuckled. "She has seen how you poke your charming nose into everything."

She grimaced as Daphne laughed and Professor Dyson appeared ill-at-ease. Mr. Randall did not seem to take notice of the discussion as he examined a piece of ceramic he had picked up from the ground.

While Professor Dyson led Neville toward the battered temple, outlining why it must have been consecrated to Juno, Priscilla ran her hand along one of the toppled columns. To touch something that had been old when the castle at Tintagel had been raised was remarkable.

Mindful of where she stepped, because she did not want to damage any artifacts yet to be uncovered, she traced the features of a woman's face, carved into a column. The body must have been broken off when the column crashed to the ground. She shivered. Had the concussion been as fierce as when the east tower fell at Shadows Fall?

Where was the rest of the carved woman? If she found the connecting piece, she might help Mr. Randall prove—or even disprove—his theory about the temple. That would be exciting and completely and safely in the past. The collapse of the tower this morning was more than enough drama for this time.

She did not see the carved woman's body in any of the columns at the top of the pile. Mayhap on the other side, she would find it. She walked around and smiled. If the light was not betraying her, she had found it. Stretching, she tried to brush dirt from it.

Her foot struck something. Not hard like a stone column or a ceramic pot. It was soft. Was something under the columns? She could not imagine what would have survived the thousands of years in this mound except stone and ceramic. Was it a beast? Some animal might have come in here seeking shelter and now cowered under the columns. It was no safer for a beast than for them. She must try to shoo it from the mound.

Bending, she looked beneath two columns propped against each other. Wide eyes met hers. Human eyes. Who was under the columns? She opened her mouth to ask that, but faltered when the eyes remained unblinking, and the man's expression did not alter.

"Sir?" She reached out to shake him.

She pulled her hand back when she saw red splashed across his face and chest. She could not breathe as she stared at the body. It was made of flesh, not of stone. It could not be a skeleton left by Romans or some ancient cult of druids. This man, if she judged by the state of the drying blood on his body, had died in the past day.

FOUR

"Put your head down toward your knees. Breathe slowly." Priscilla spoke the words with a serenity she could not feel. More hysterics would be useless. She had heard enough screams of fright and horror when she revealed what she had found beneath the columns. "Slowly, Professor. Breathe slowly."

"Here, my lady," said Mr. Randall, holding out a damp cloth.

Thanking him, she folded the cold compress against Professor Dyson's forehead. The professor had almost swooned at the sight of the man's body. Priscilla understood his reaction, because her own stomach was none too steady. She was grateful her daughters were made of sterner stuff. Leah had been more than a little exasperated when Daphne had led her from the mound to return to Shadows Fall.

"Watch him, Mr. Randall," she ordered. "Keep telling him to breathe slowly."

"What are we going to do?"

"Wait for the constable. Daphne will send for him."

"Constable?" Mr. Randall's face became ruddy, then as gray as the dead man's.

"It is what one does when one finds a corpse," Neville

said as he came around the stack of columns. "Do you know the man's identity?"

"No! No!" shrieked Professor Dyson, jumping to his feet. "We have nothing to do with this. You cannot blame us for someone else's heinous act."

Priscilla glanced at Mr. Randall, who urged the professor to sit again on a fallen column. As soon as he had persuaded the older man to breathe slowly and hold the cloth to his forehead, she repeated Neville's question.

Mr. Randall shook his head. "I have never seen the man before."

"He is wearing a strange ring on the forefinger of his left hand. It appears to be made of tin and is engraved with what might be a wave on the sea or the letter *C.*"

"I have never seen a ring like that." Mr. Randall looked at the professor. "Neither of us have."

"Hmm . . ." Neville walked back toward the body.

"He does not seem convinced." Mr. Randall's voice rose on each word.

Not wanting to cope with two panicked men, Priscilla said in her most soothing voice, "He is not accusing you or the professor of any misdeed, Mr. Randall. He is trying to sort out facts from conjecture, much as you do with the artifacts you uncover."

"Oh, I see."

Priscilla wished she could say the same. Who would kill a man among these ruins? Walking to where Neville was studying the body as intently as Mr. Randall had studied the piece of pottery, she asked that question.

"Someone who wished the body to be found," Neville said with a cool smile. "That is the obvious answer, Pris."

"Obvious answers are not always the right answer."

"True, but it is a theory which I believe will prove

correct." He pointed to marks in the dirt. "The body was dragged here and set where it could be found quite easily."

"Dragged from where?"

"That is a good question." Standing, he looked past her. "Our footprints have obliterated any sign of whether the man was killed within the mound or if he was murdered outside and brought here to give the killer a chance to put some distance between himself and the constable before the body was found."

"Him? You are assuming the murderer was a man?"

A smile tugged at his expressive mouth. "I know we both are aware that some women are capable of murder, but whoever dragged the corpse was very strong." He kicked at the ground. "The dirt is loose from the professor's work, which would make it more difficult to pull the body across it."

"You always preceive the most important things, which I would be wise not to ask how you learned."

"Common sense this time, Pris. Just as it is common sense to assume this man died from a blow to the skull. Although his chest is covered with blood, there is a dent in his head."

"I wonder if this is related to the tower's collapse."

He scowled. "We have one real murder. We do not need to cloud the circumstances with supposition."

"But we must consider all the facts. I—"

Someone rushed in. Priscilla was about to greet the constable, then realized the lad was too young for such duties. His straw-colored hair sprouted in every possible direction, and a fuzz of the same color covered his chin and cheeks. His clothes were worn and, even from where she stood, stank.

"Professor Dyson! Professor Dyson!" The lad ran

straight toward the distraught man. "Look what I found!"

The professor's head jerked up. "What is it, Seth?"

"Look at this!"

The flagon Seth held was large enough to hold several quarts of wine. Save for a chip in its narrow opening, the stone jar was perfect. Like the pot Professor Dyson had showed them before, this appeared none the worse for its centuries beneath the earth.

Standing, the professor took the flagon and ran his fingers along the embossed relief of full-chested horses on it. "Where did you find it?"

"On the beach below Shadows Fall."

"The beach?" Neville asked, and the lad turned to stare at him. "How often does something like this wash up on shore?"

"I don't know," Seth replied.

Neville plucked the flagon from the professor's hands. Shaking water off it, he ignored the gasps of dismay from the other three men. He turned so Priscilla could see it as well. "A nice find, Seth."

"How did the flagon escape being smashed against the rocks?" she asked.

"I don't know," Seth answered again when the professor and Mr. Randall looked at him. "I found it, and I remembered you saying to bring anything we found to you, Professor, and you would pay us well."

"You found it on the beach?" Priscilla asked.

The lad looked at her as if she had taken a knock in the cradle. "Yes. It was sitting at the water's edge, and there were two others off to one side." He smiled. "Like they were waiting for me! It *is* beautiful, isn't it? I hid the other two so nobody else will take them, Professor. A shilling each, right?"

"Yes, yes," the professor said. "Pay him, Randall."

While his assistant was finding the proper coins for the lad, the professor took the flagon from Neville. He examined it with a proprietary smile, and Priscilla wondered who was funding this excavation. Whoever it was would expect such fine pieces to be turned over to him or her. From the expression on Professor Dyson's face, she suspected not all the pieces would be given to his patron.

Seth left with instructions to bring the other two flagons to the cottage the professor was using in Trepoole, but Professor Dyson did not give the lad the one he held. It did not seem to bother Seth, for his shouts as he raced across the field revealed his excitement with the largesse.

"This is incredible, Randall!" the professor crowed. "Have you ever seen its like? And two more! Who knows what else we will find?"

Neville scowled. "The rest of your treasure hunt may be delayed while the murder is investigated."

"Murder?" Professor Dyson staggered as if Neville had given him a facer. "Oh, dear me! I forgot about the murder." He folded up, sitting again.

Mr. Randall took the flagon and held it close to his chest. The professor hid his face again as he shook his head and groaned.

The interior darkened slightly, and Priscilla looked toward the door. A tall, broad-shouldered silhouette almost filled it. As the man stepped onto the mound, she saw his hair was a pale brown and his riding clothes well made. His boots showed they had enjoyed much attention from his valet. He carried a riding crop under his arm. His face was lined with age and streaks of gray glistened in his hair where the sun touched it, and she guessed he was of a similar age to her aunt.

"Professor Dyson," he said, his bass voice reverberating through the mound, "you look as if you have lost your most treasured artifact. What is wrong?"

The professor moaned.

The man in the doorway took the flagon from Mr. Randall and regarded it with a smile.

"Who are you?" Neville asked.

The man regarded him with an icy glare and an insolent sneer. "I am Robert Beddlemere. Who are *you*?"

"I am your neighbor." His expression became as arrogant as Lord Beddlemere's. "Neville Hathaway." He put his hand on Priscilla's arm. "Lady Priscilla Flanders, my fiancée."

Joy rushed through her at his choice of words, for she had not been introduced before as his betrothed, but Priscilla suppressed it. A man was dead. This was no time to consider her happiness.

"Hathaway?" asked Lord Beddlemere with another superior smile. "I had heard you were coming to take up residence at Shadows Fall. Its condition must be quite a shock for a man accustomed to the comforts of London."

"There is nothing that cannot be repaired, even the east tower, now that I am turning my attention to it."

Priscilla watched the marquess's face at Neville's words, which suggested he had had many more important matters to consider before coming to Cornwall. Lord Beddlemere frowned, then his smile returned as he shifted the flagon to his left hand and held out his right.

"That house has been too empty too long." He chuckled. "Except for the ghosts reputed to be haunting it in search of vengeance for the violence done to them."

"Is that why you believe they are ghosts?" Neville asked.

"That is one hypothesis. It is said, and Professor Dyson can confirm the belief has held true through many different cultures and times, that a violent death makes it impossible for a soul to rest until it has obtained its revenge against its murderer and its murderer's descendants."

"Then I shall need to make room for one more phantom on my lands."

Lord Beddlemere's brow furrowed. "What do you mean?"

"This." Neville stepped aside, drawing Priscilla with him.

When she saw the marquess's eyes widen as he stared at the corpse and reeled back a half step, she wanted to chide Neville for resorting to dramatics. Lord Beddlemere could have been told a bit more gently. Going to the marquess, she put her hand on his arm and guided him toward where Professor Dyson was still holding his head in his hands.

"Thank you, my lady," Lord Beddlemere said, "but I wish to see this dead man more closely."

"You are almost as pale as the corpse."

"From the initial shock. I am recovering myself." He seemed rather perturbed that she had seen his momentary weakness.

"We have sent for the constable."

His nose wrinkled. "Kliskey? The man is incapable of catching a poacher. What makes you think he can do anything here?"

"This man is unlikely to run," Neville said without a hint of amusement.

Lord Beddlemere faltered, then laughed. "You have a strange outlook on the world, Hathaway. Mayhap that is an asset at a time like this."

"Do you recognize the man?"

"I believe I might have seen him in Trepoole, but I am not certain."

"The constable may know."

The marquess shook his head. "If you are depending on Kliskey to help much beyond giving a name to the corpse, you shall be disappointed."

Priscilla found herself agreeing with Lord Beddlemere's assessment when the constable arrived almost two hours later. Constable Kliskey was a man of advanced years, or so he appeared, for his face was weathered. His hands quivered as he bent to examine the corpse. From palsy or from fear?

"This is Gab Moyle." The constable's voice shook as hard as his hands.

"Gab Moyle?" Professor Dyson came to his feet. "That thief! He has been lurking around this excavation site." He clenched his fists. "I warned him to stay away." His face became ashen. "Not that I had a hand in the man's death. Tell them, Randall."

Mr. Randall said softly, "The professor would not kill a man, especially—" He gulped. "Especially one as strong as this man was."

"You must not think I had a hand in this!" cried the professor. He swayed on his feet.

"Mr. Randall," Lord Beddlemere said quietly, "mayhap it would be for the best if you took Professor Dyson back to your cottage, so he might compose himself after this ordeal."

Neville frowned. "The man was found at his excavation. Dyson needs to share what he knows. Randall, too."

"They will, I am sure." Lord Beddlemere gave the two men a sympathetic smile. "Keeping the professor here now will not help any investigation."

Even Neville had to agree when the professor opened his mouth, then fell face-first into the dirt. Mr. Randall roused the professor and took him to the cart they had driven to the site. Priscilla feared Professor Dyson would swoon again on every step, but Mr. Randall got him into the cart. Only when they drove away did she realize that the flagon had been left behind and that Lord Beddlemere still held it.

"What sort of man was Gab Moyle?" asked Neville as the cart bounced out of the field and onto the road.

Constable Kliskey gnawed on his lower lip while he looked to Lord Beddlemere.

"Tell Sir Neville what you know, man!" ordered the marquess.

"You are Sir Neville?" The constable swallowed hard.

Lord Beddlemere shook his head. "I introduced you to him and Lady Priscilla when you came in here. Use your brain for once, Kliskey!"

"Yes, my lord." Constable Kliskey stared at the dead man. "Gab Moyle lives near Trepoole, and he fishes."

"He just fished?" Neville leaned one elbow on a broken column.

His nonchalance must have unsettled the constable more, because Constable Kliskey tripped over his words as he said, "You know how—you know how things are here. In Cornwall, I mean, sir." He looked at the marquess. "Not on your estate, my lord."

"We are on Hathaway's lands here," Lord Beddlemere said with relief.

"I don't mean any insult to either of you gentlemen, but you need to understand. Things are rough along the shore. Men do . . ." He took a deep breath. "Men do what they need to in order to provide for themselves and their families."

"So he might have been involved with smugglers?"

"I don't know about such things, sir."

Priscilla put her hand on Neville's arm as he drew in a deep breath. Castigating the constable for failing to do his job would do nothing to help them discover who had laid Mr. Moyle so low and left his body in the mound. Neville's frown told her that he would have enjoyed reminding the constable of his duties, but he nodded.

"Constable Kliskey," she said, "you should have the body removed to where the coroner can examine it. Mr. Moyle's family needs to be told the sad news."

"I can do that." The constable stiffened his shoulders. "I will speak to the vicar at St. Anthony's about the burial. Would that be all right?"

"That would be quite proper, constable." She gave him her best smile, and the man relaxed. Had he thought he would be blamed for the death? Even Neville's exasperation was because Constable Kliskey seemed unwilling to do what needed to be done. "Have the vicar let us know when the services will be and if we can do anything to help."

"What help?"

"My late husband was a vicar and I know how burdensome an unexpected death can be to a village."

"Is that so?" The constable recalled himself—or mayhap Neville's scowl reminded him of his manners—because he added, "I will inform Reverend Mr. Rosewarne, my lady."

"Thank you." She looked once more at the dead man. "I believe there is nothing we can do here. If you have any questions, Constable Kliskey, please call at Shadows Fall. It was a pleasure to make your acquaintance, Lord Beddlemere, although I wish it had been under different circumstances."

He bowed over her hand. "Good day, my lady." He looked past her. "Hathaway, I trust we can count on your cooperation in this matter."

"Yes, you can count on cooperation from both of us."

"Both?" The marquess gulped, and his face reddened. "I did not guess—that is, I assumed Lady Priscilla would not want more to do with this jumble."

"I doubt you could keep her out of it." Neville smiled as he offered his arm to her. "Good afternoon, Beddlemere. I trust you will see the flagon is returned to the professor."

"Of course." He scowled.

Priscilla had barely followed Neville out the door before she heard the marquess chastising the constable. She was tempted to tell Lord Beddlemere that such derogatory words were not likely to inspire the constable to do more.

As she walked with Neville toward the stile, she looked back at the field. "Don't you find it odd that the temple is barely damaged? It is as if the mound were built up over the temple to protect it."

"I've been thinking, too, that it is amazing the temple survived as well as it did."

"Good, and your conclusion, Professor Hathaway?"

He chuckled. "None yet." He handed her over the stile. "Are you saying someone manipulated this site?

Mayhap the druids built the mound to keep their own gods from warring with the heretic Romans."

"The next thing you will be saying is that the Roman gods were furious over Professor Dyson's intrusion and struck Mr. Moyle dead."

He jumped down beside her. "That is farfetched, Pris. If the gods were going to be angry, don't you think they would have punished the professor and Randall?"

"They may have indirectly. I cannot imagine they will be continuing here."

Resting his foot on the stone wall, he stared across the field. "If I had not met Constable Kliskey myself, I would have to agree with you, Pris. However, I doubt the good constable will consider halting the excavation."

"But there may be clues."

"There *are* clues. There always are clues. I doubt Kliskey will find them."

"So you and I must."

He grinned at her. "I was hoping you would say that, Pris."

FIVE

Lady Cordelia was a woman who should never be kept waiting for an answer. Neville was well aware of that. Even if he had not been, the lady's glower and the tap of her toe against the parlor floor would have warned him of the dangers of allowing her temper to escalate into rage.

"The constable?" Lady Cordelia demanded as she gave her niece her sternest look. "Priscilla, I had hoped that, in journeying to this desolate place, one good thing would occur. I had hoped you would put aside your predilection for appalling deaths."

"It was not my wish to be involved in another murder investigation." Priscilla sat between her daughters with her hands folded in her lap. At first glance, she appeared as serene as if she were discussing plans for tea, but Neville noticed how tightly her fingers were clasped. "However, I cannot pretend I did not find Mr. Moyle's corpse."

Lady Cordelia put her hands over her ears. "Refrain from saying such things, Priscilla. I lament the thought of what will be said when the *ton* discovers you are involved—yet again—in such a low pursuit."

"Do you consider the pursuit of truth low?" asked Neville, earning a frown from both Priscilla and her aunt. He would not stand silent while Priscilla was being dressed down.

"You are welcome to play your word games else-where." Lady Cordelia's tone could have frozen the sun. "If you have any concern for Priscilla's future—"

"I have made my concerns quite well known."

Priscilla said, "Neville, there is no need to whip up a tired horse."

He did not release his chuckle. Although Priscilla despised her aunt's penchant for pointing out every mistake she believed Priscilla had made since the last scold, she accepted them as an inevitable part of her aunt's company. Even he had to own that Lady Cordelia's anxiety arose from her affection for Priscilla and the children.

He knew that, but he could not be so forgiving. "If you would allow me to finish, Pris . . ."

Her aunt muttered something, probably the same thing she said each time she heard him address Priscilla that way. He had yet to figure out what she was saying, and he believed himself wise not to investigate too closely. So far, he had not uttered anything that Priscilla could not persuade her aunt to disregard. If Lady Cordelia was not so beloved by Priscilla, he would have spoken his true thoughts to the old tough months ago.

"Do say what you feel you *must,* Neville," Priscilla said, and he heard her warning. Riling her aunt further would be foolish.

"I *must* say that I agree with you, Lady Cordelia."

"You do?" Lady Cordelia's toe stopped tapping.

"Priscilla has been connected with too many of these crimes in recent months."

"That is what I was saying." Her frown eased. "Mayhap you can make her see sense."

He tried to halt his reaction. It was impossible not to laugh, for he had never guessed Lady Cordelia would plead with *him* to help change Priscilla's mind.

The lady stared at him, then strode out of the room, outrage like a burning aura around her.

Priscilla rose. "That was rude, Neville. You owe her an apology."

"I tried not to laugh, Pris. I really did."

Daphne giggled. "It was funny to hear Aunt Cordelia ask for Uncle Neville's help."

"It was startling," Priscilla said, smiling. "Neville, you must apologize to her. If she leaves Shadows Fall, we will have no choice but to go as well."

Dash it! He had let himself forget Priscilla could not remain beneath his roof without a proper watchdog. Her daughters were too young to act as chaperones, and the servants were unacceptable in the eyes of the Polite World. Mayhap he should return to Town and obtain a special license or persuade her to elope with him to Gretna Green. He knew Priscilla would be hurt by either suggestion, because she wanted to be married at St. Julian's in London. He did, as well. It had been Lazarus's last church and he liked the idea of his friend's spirit being there during their wedding.

Spirit. Now *he* was thinking about ghosts and noises in the night. If he was not careful, he would let Priscilla persuade him that the tower falling had been an attempt on his life.

"When next I speak with your aunt, I will tell her how much I regret my laughter," he said.

"And nothing more?"

"Pris, don't you trust me to have some discretion?"

"You are the most discreet man I have ever met." She

put her hands on his arms. "No one else keeps so many secrets."

"Secrets?"

"Of things past."

"They are not secret, but things I would rather not recall."

Leah bounced over to him. "Illicit things?"

"Whatever gave you that idea?" he asked.

"Aunt Cordelia said once that you were caught doing—"

"Enough," Priscilla said. "You have your sums to complete, Leah, and Daphne agreed to help you with that embroidery stitch you have not yet mastered."

"Must I do it now?"

"Yes."

Neville withheld his laugh until the girls left the room. Even so, it earned him another frown from Priscilla. She was not vexed with him. She was distressed by Moyle's murder.

As if he had said that aloud, she said, "Ennis told me Mr. Moyle had a wife and seven children. You need to give them a look-in, Neville."

"I want to speak to Mrs. Moyle about any enemies her husband might have had and about his recent activities."

"You need to offer her comfort." She smiled sadly. "That duty you inherited along with this estate. The village and the living at St. Anthony's are your obligations."

"I doubt if anyone in the village has high expectations of support from the Hathaways."

"Mayhap not in the past, but you will do your duty for them."

He grimaced. "Who would have guessed *I* would be

responsible for the welfare of a village and the living at a church?"

"Life has given you an interesting path, hasn't it?"

"Going to comfort Moyle's widow is not something I shall do well."

"Nonsense. You will do fine."

"Will you come with me, Pris?"

She nodded, then went to where Stoddard had left the wine and glasses. Pouring the wine, she handed one glass to him. He took a sip and, grimacing, lifted her glass from her hand.

"It is sour, Pris."

"I know how it feels." She rubbed her forehead. "I am tempted to heed Aunt Cordelia and leave Cornwall without looking back."

Slipping his arm around her, he leaned her head against his shoulder. "If you go, who will help me pick out the colors for the rest of the house? I assume you would rather not have the whole of it painted red."

"May I see the rest of the house?"

"It is in sorrowful condition."

"I know." She stepped away from him. "Looking about, however, may help me take my mind off what I saw on that mound."

"Can you?"

"Of course not." Priscilla went to the door and looked across the stairs to the portraits lining the wall. She flinched when something brushed her leg, then realized it was a cat. Squatting to scratch behind its ear, she stood when Neville spoke her name.

She turned and gasped. She had not realized how close he was standing to her. Although she longed to get lost in his eyes, she avoided looking into them. The sympathy in them would undo the fragile wall around her emotions.

"Shall I show you some of the better parts of Shadows Fall?" His voice was so measured she knew he understood what she did not dare to speak.

"That would be lovely."

When he offered his arm, she let him draw her fingers within it. He began naming the people in the portraits they passed.

"I am impressed, Neville, that you are so versed in your family's hsitory."

"Don't be. I am reading the names affixed to the frames, and I can guess when each person lived by their clothes."

"Your family seems very fond of cats. It is a challenge to keep them away from Aunt Cordelia."

"Do you think we are up to such a challenge?"

"I know no one better than you to handle such a task, Neville. Surely you have done deeds as daring when you were in the theater."

He laughed. "You have no idea, Pris."

"Someday, you must share those tales with me."

"The ones suitable for your ears . . . mayhap."

Priscilla smiled as she walked with Neville up the narrow, winding stairs. Her fingers brushed the railing, which was smooth from many hands before hers. Looking at the stained-glass window splashing shades of red and blue into the upper corridor, she took a deep breath. She wondered how many others had climbed this staircase and enjoyed the close, heated scent of this sun-warmed passage. Pausing at the top of the stairs, she squinted through the shaft of sunlight piercing deep into the shadowed hallway.

"We cannot explore it all before it gets dark," Neville said.

"I know, but it is easy to get caught up in imagining what Shadows Fall can become. It must once have been glorious."

"It was." He tapped the frame of another portrait, this one of a man with a ruff high under his chin. "This is Sir Pawley Hathaway, who purchased these lands when the monasteries were dissolved. From what I can piece together, he built the house from the ruins of the monastery."

"Casting the brothers out into the secular world."

He laughed. "I suspect they went quite willingly when their other choice was dying."

"Neville, you are a cynic."

"On the contrary." He ran his finger along the frame, then brushed the thick fuzz of dust onto his coat. "I believe one should always take advantage of one's current situation, as my predecessors did. Somehow, the Hathaways were in the right place to obtain this property, and then they were wise enough to keep it—and their heads—during the upheaval to follow."

"If you represent the attributes of your ancestors, that is no surprise." She smiled. "Mayhap they kept cats as a reminder of how important it is for one always to land on one's feet."

"Or to smell out rats."

She laughed as they continued along the upper corridor. Unlike below, this passage did not reek. A broken window at the end had allowed debris in at the same time it kept the air fresh.

Neville had not been jesting when he said the house needed much work. It would take a score of craftsmen many years to repair the damage she had seen. The idea of having their betrothal ball at Shadows Fall in such a short time seemed ludicrous, but she did not say that. Neville would see her words as a challenge and become even more determined to have the house ready.

Going to the window, Priscilla looked out. Her heart thudded when she saw the shattered tower below. If Neville and the footman had not left the tower when they had, both of them would be dead.

"Pris, we are safe," Neville said, putting his hands on her shoulders.

"Are we?"

"It is unlike you to be pessimistic."

"I am not being pessimistic. I am fearful for you."

He turned her to face him. "I appreciate your concern, Pris, but you need to focus on the real dangers to me."

"And those are?" she asked, smiling as he did.

"Your aunt's schemes to banish me to China or farther."

She laughed as they went down another staircase. He led the way to a heavy oak door. Bowing, he ushered her into what remained of a ballroom. It once had been beautiful, for hints of gilt and plaster remained on the curved walls. A minstrel's gallery was carved with mythical animals, and the stone floor was smooth beneath her feet. Chandeliers paraded along the center of the room. Five chandeliers! Sunlight poured through broken windowpanes to dance on tarnished bronze. All the windows were high in the wall, but the wind had found its way in, depositing dried leaves, and clumps of dirt were piled against the hearth across from the minstrels' gallery. Odors of damp and neglect assailed her. Along the walls, squeaks warned of rodent trespassers.

Neville went toward the back corner, and she saw a

stairwell leading up to the next floor. He put his hand on the unadorned newel post. A chunk fell to the floor, barely missing his boot.

"The walls are well built." Priscilla tried to shake the banister. It did not move, although so many of the supports were cracked their original pattern was lost. "A good cleaning will make a big difference."

"So you don't think I would be wiser to raze the whole and begin anew?"

"I gave that idea some thought, but no, there are lovely parts of this house." She ran her fingers along the banister. "Neville, why were you in such a hurry to paint the walls downstairs?"

"I thought the family portraits should be the only artwork visible when your daughters arrived. The murals would have been very . . . hmm, mayhap enlightening is not the right word. Educational?"

She stared at him, then laughed. "The murals could not have been that salacious."

"One of my recent ancestors had a taste for debauchery, at least on the walls." Looking around, he said, "I believe this room can be made presentable in time for the ball."

"You want to hold it *here*?"

"Why not?" His nose wrinkled when he kicked his way through a pile of leaves as he crossed toward thick drapes beside the hearth. Behind them were tall windows like those in the ruined solar. "I was a bit optimistic to believe Shadows Fall would be ready for guests, but they have already been invited."

She rubbed her palm against one of the diamond-shaped windowpanes so she could see out. "Did you know the condition of the house when you suggested holding the betrothal ball here?"

"I had my suspicions it would not be in the best condition."

Looking out at the whitecaps frosting the sea, she laughed. "There must be a reason why you wished to host an assembly within these ruined walls."

"Several. Your aunt, for one."

"My aunt?" She turned and discovered he had come to stand right behind her again. Smiling, she said, "You have befuddled me even more."

"Lady Cordelia believes me incapable of making a single correct decision."

"No, she believes that of me." She put her hands on his waistcoat, stroking the rough fabric. "She believes you incapable of anything but roguery, but neither explains why you wanted to hold the betrothal party here."

"I want to show her I can be right."

"You expect to have this house in order in time for the ball?"

He spun her about as if he could hear the music of a country dance. "Do you think I will miss the chance to show the whole world—Polite and otherwise—that you have agreed to be my wife?"

"My dearest Neville, no one will believe you allowed yourself to be leg-shackled until we have celebrated our tenth anniversary."

Laughing, he drew her closer. "Such language! If you speak with that Town cant in Stonehall-on-Sea, I suspect a matron or two will be quite scandalized."

"You mistake my habits for yours." She locked her fingers behind his neck. "Neville, you are certain to vex Aunt Cordelia further if you are successful."

"Mayhap, but she will have to own that I am capable of taking care of her favorite niece."

"I am her only niece."

"Which proves my point."

Kissing him lightly, she said, "You are incorrigible."

"Thank you, my lady."

"I did not mean it as a compliment." She stepped back and looked around the room. "If the missing windowpanes are replaced and the floor swept and only the center trio of chandeliers are lit, it is possible the guests will not notice the peeling paint and missing sections of plaster."

"Now you are getting the idea." He went to the hearth. Bending down, he looked into the chimney. "I shall have a fire laid to check if there are any blockages or nests."

"A little smoke will not harm the room further."

"And getting rid of nests may get rid of the noise you heard last night."

"So you believe me on that score at least."

"Of course." Coming to his feet, he rested one hand on the high mantel. "Pris, I will check about and see if anyone else heard anything."

"Thank you." She frowned. "If that offer is an attempt to distract me from other matters—"

"Not directly." He drew her closer. "This is a much more pleasant diversion." His arm swept around her, tugging her against him. His mouth slanted across hers. He did not hurry, but explored her lips fully. Sensations flowed within her, potent and dangerous. His other arm slipped around her shoulders, and her fingers slid up his back.

She opened her eyes, and she traced the strong planes of his face. The black hair edging his temples gleamed in the sunlight far less brightly than the glow in his eyes. Her finger traveled along his well-sculptured nose before reaching the fullness of his lips, which brought thrilling pleasure to her.

She smiled as he kissed her. She wanted more than that teasing kiss. With her hand against the back of his head, she steered his mouth to hers. As her lips softened beneath his tender assault, his tongue caressed hers before luring it to sample the recesses of his mouth. His accelerated breath mingled with hers; then his lips sparked delight across her face and along her neck. Her fingers tightened on his back.

When he whispered her name against her ear, Priscilla pulled herself away. Not at his whisper, but at a sound from the other side of the ballroom. She saw Stoddard in the doorway. The butler wore no expression.

"Yes?" asked Neville as he kept his arm around her waist.

"A caller for you, sir."

Neville's brow furrowed. "A caller? Here? Who is it?"

"She gave her name as Lady Barbara Garroway."

"Lady Barbara?" asked Priscilla, astonished.

"Do you know her, Pris?"

"Yes." Looking at Stoddard, she said, "Please ask Lady Barbara to wait for us in the parlor."

He bowed his head and left.

When she took a deep breath and let it go slowly, Neville touched her cheek and asked, "What is it, Pris? Why do you feel the need to gird your loins before greeting Lady Barbara?"

"Please refrain from speaking so in her hearing. She would have a fit of the vapors."

"I shall endeavor to restrain myself."

"You need to." She glanced toward the door and

sighed. "Lady Barbara Garroway is Aunt Cordelia's dearest bosom bow."

What he said, she hoped he would not repeat in either lady's hearing, but the oath was the same one she had been thinking as soon as she heard Lady Barbara's name. Matters were going from bad to worse.

SIX

Priscilla should not have been surprised when they reached the parlor to discover it was empty. Lady Barbara must have insisted on being taken to Aunt Cordelia.

"Mayhap we should go to your aunt's room to greet Lady Barbara," Neville said in a tone that revealed he wanted to do no such thing.

Taking pity on him and herself, she smiled. "Such an action would suggest that we do not trust them."

"Do you?"

"Yes." She laughed. "I trust them to look for ways to persuade me that I am making the biggest mistake of my life." Her smile vanished. "Once Aunt Cordelia tells Lady Barbara about the murder at the excavation site, she is certain to want to go there posthaste."

"Why?"

"She fancies herself an equal to any man at Bow Street in solving crimes."

"Is she their equal? If she is, we could use her help."

Priscilla shook her head. "The only crime she has ever solved was when her abigail mixed up handkerchiefs in the wash."

He grimaced. "Dash it, Pris! An amateur sleuth is the very last thing we need now."

"Are you saying we are not amateurs?"

"You know what I mean."

She put her hand on his arm. "I do know what you mean. I suppose we should wait here."

Going to the stairs, he shouted over the railing. A footman Priscilla did not recognize hurried up the steps and nodded when Neville ordered some wine—"Some good wine, not the vinegar served earlier."—to be brought.

The footman delivered two dusty bottles of wine to the parlor and waited while Neville sampled each. The footman could not hide his grin when Neville told him to get rid of all the bottles decanted earlier. He had a bounce in his step as he left the room.

"You may end up with foxed footmen," Priscilla said when Neville handed her a glass of wine.

"If they can drink that disgusting swill, they are better men than I."

"Or less discriminating."

"Dash it, Pris. You are irritating when you are right."

"You should be accustomed to it by now, because I have been right on many occasions."

He draped an arm around her shoulders. "You need not remind me how many times your mind has been more discerning than mine."

Priscilla's answer was halted when she heard, "Lady Barbara Garroway, sir."

Stoddard's tone suggested he would rather announce the old gentleman in black himself rather than another woman who was certain to find fault in everything his staff did.

"Be pleasant, Neville," Priscilla said as they turned to face the door.

"Aren't I always?" he whispered.

She had an answer she could not speak as her aunt guided her friend into the room, followed by Daphne and Leah, who were well aware of the fireworks that could happen. She hoped Neville would heed her. Infuriating Aunt Cordelia *and* her friend was a guarantee of more trouble at Shadows Fall.

Lady Barbara Garroway never missed an opportunity to make an entrance. She was an elegant woman and tall, with a full bosom emphasized by elegant lace on her dark green bodice. Her hair was as dark as Neville's and laced with strands of pure white. Lady Barbara would not accept having a mediocre gray in her hair. Handsome, rather than beautiful, she wore her family's prominence like a jewel to match the ones at her throat and glittering across her fingers. She was a woman who refused to be ignored, and she reveled in being the focus of all eyes.

Her entrance was ruined when a black-and-white cat slithered around her ankles. Aunt Cordelia let out a shriek and cried, "Get that loathsome beast out of the house!" She sneezed.

Stoddard scooped up the offending feline and backed out of the room. He shooed another away with his foot, and his call of, "Kitty, kitty, kitty," filled the room until his voice faded into the distance.

"I had forgotten your weakness around cats, Cordelia," Lady Barbara said with a superior smile. Crossing the room, she gave Priscilla a quick kiss on either cheek. Lady Barbara made no secret that she preferred the ways of the Continent and acted as if Napoleon had chosen to build an empire solely to vex her.

"My dear, how lovely you look," Lady Barbara gushed. "You were wan when I last saw you."

"That was at my husband's funeral."

"Ah, yes." Lady Barbara shrugged off her faux pas, and Priscilla hoped she would be as forgiving of anything Neville or the children might blurt out. "That must have been just about a year ago, right?" She looked from Priscilla to Neville.

"Almost two years," she replied coolly at the suggestion she had cut short her mourning to accept Neville's offer.

"That explains why these girls have grown so much." She took Daphne by the shoulders and hugged her so hard Daphne gasped. "Every time I look at you, I cannot believe you are old enough to be fired off. How thrilled your father would have been to see how pretty you are!"

Priscilla was about to respond, then realized Lady Barbara had been speaking to Aunt Cordelia, who bustled over and began to exclaim about Daphne's golden hair and youthful skin. Priscilla must take care not to let the two older women rile her to the point of saying the very thing that would offer them an opportunity to focus their comments on Neville. He could defend himself quite well, but that would infuriate her aunt and Lady Barbara even more.

Motioning for Leah to come over to her, which her daughter did eagerly, Priscilla asked, "Are you and your sister all right?"

"Was the man really dead, Mama?"

She nodded.

"Then I do not understand why you sent us away. I want to help you and Uncle Neville capture the murderer."

"Murderer, did you say?" asked Lady Barbara. "Have I missed something exciting?" She frowned at Aunt

Cordelia as if her friend had conspired to keep her from knowing the latest *on dits*.

Instead of answering, Neville lifted her hand and bowed over it. "Welcome to Shadows Fall, Lady Barbara. I do hope you will excuse the mess my family left us."

She laughed with a merry lilt that suggested she was as young as Priscilla. Barbara was at least two decades older. When she eyed Neville in an obvious appraisal, Aunt Cordelia frowned and hooked her arm through Barbara's. She led her friend from the room, talking so low and fast that Priscilla could not guess what pap Aunt Cordelia was filling her friend's head with. Aunt Cordelia was furious that her niece had been—in her opinion—taken in by Neville's smooth patter. She would not allow her bosom bow to be bamboozled as well.

"That is a dreary expression on your face, Pris," Neville said, refilling her glass as her daughters watched their elders and giggled. "Could you be jealous of the warm glance yon dowager gave me?"

"After a comment like that, I should leave you to her wiles."

His brows rose in mock horror. "Do say you will save me from such a fate."

"A fate worse than death?"

Putting the bottle back on the tray, he said, abruptly somber, "I never have understood the meaning of that phrase. What could be worse than death and the surcease of all hope?"

"I would prefer not to think of it."

He nodded. "As would I, but it is a reality for Moyle and his family. A reality that will not go away until we discover who killed him and why."

* * *

Neville tried to rid himself of his bleak mood by the time dinner was ready. That Lady Cordelia insisted they dress for the evening meal, which he would have preferred to eat off a tray while chatting with Priscilla and her daughters, added to his dismals. She had further commanded that the meal be served in a setting that met with her approval. The edict had sent the household into a flurry of activity, trying to clean a small dining chamber that had been inhabited by birds and vermin for the past quarter century.

Tugging at the cravat he had tied too tightly in his annoyance, Neville walked into the room his butler and housekeeper had chosen. He paused in the arched doorway and smiled.

The room, which was buzzing like a beehive as servants rushed about following Mrs. Crosby's orders, was almost as large as the parlor. A pair of hearths mirrored each other at opposite ends of the room. A carved screen arched up to the high ceiling, the wooden animals upon it looking as if they were climbing a dark brown rainbow. More paintings were hung on the walls between two bays of double windows, each taller than he was. Unlike all the others he had seen, these pictures depicted the sea and the fields around Shadows Fall.

In the center of the stone floor, a carpet he had noticed in one of the upper rooms had been spread beneath a table that was long enough to seat the guests at one of Prinny's parties. It was of aged oak, as were the chairs marching along both sides of it. The black velvet covering the seats had been brushed clean of dust and cat hair.

On the table a trio of candelabra were placed at equal distances from each other. They were silver, and he saw streaks where they had been hastily polished. Seven place settings were waiting at the table.

Seven? Who else was joining them for dinner? He would learn soon enough. Odd that Priscilla had not mentioned anyone else, but mayhap another guest had arrived early for the betrothal ball. He hoped the rest would take their time traveling to Cornwall, giving his household a chance to make more bedrooms habitable.

A footman was stepping down from a ladder as Mrs. Crosby watched with her arms crossed in front of her. She went to the gold draperies and adjusted its folds to her satisfaction. Pushing aside one, she pulled out a cat of almost the same color and gave it a gentle shove toward one of the footmen, who quickly picked it up. He yelped as the cat scratched him in an effort to escape, but he hurried to carry it out a door that led to the kitchen.

"That will do, I suppose," Mrs. Crosby said to no one in particular.

"It looks fine," Neville replied as he walked into the room. "In fact, I daresay, you and your staff should be labeled as miracle workers, Mrs. Crosby."

The housekeeper flushed, tittering like a young miss overmastered by a beau. "That is kind of you to say, sir."

"It is the truth." He looked at the table and the china, which had a royal purple and gold design. "Where did you find those dishes, Mrs. Crosby?"

"In storage rooms over the kitchen. There are crates and crates up there, so we were lucky to find these in the second box we opened." Her nose wrinkled. "The first was filled with cloth that crumbled when we touched it."

"Once we get more of the house suitable for guests,

I suspect Lady Priscilla would like to explore those crates to discover if there is anything else worth saving."

"Stoddard told me the attics are full of boxes, both here in the house and over the stables."

He smiled. The possibility of finding treasure would excite Leah, who hoped to see a pirate ship flying skull and crossbones sail into the cove. While he and Priscilla concerned themselves with finding who had slain Gab Moyle—and tried to keep Lady Barbara from interfering—her daughters could explore. Lady Cordelia might be willing to oversee them while she determined what was worth keeping and what was ruined beyond repair.

The footsteps behind him were so light he would not have noticed, save that his ears were listening for these particular footfalls. He turned, his smile broadening as he drew in the splendid sight of Priscilla walking toward him.

She was dressed in her best to satisfy her aunt and Lady Barbara. Priscilla always looked lovely, whether she was mucking about in the dirt of a churchyard, seeking clues to a bodysnatcher, or costumed for the merriment of a medieval fair. With her luxurious blond hair piled in soft curls and entwined with silver and gold ribbons, a few strands remained free over her forehead and around her ears. She wore only the simple gold chain he had given her around her neck. It disappeared beneath the modest neckline of her pale blue dress. At its end, where it could rest directly over her heart, was the wedding ring Lazarus had given her.

How many years had he loved her, Neville wondered. He had known her since shortly after Lazarus asked her to marry, and he had seen from the beginning how perfect Priscilla was for his friend. Like Lazarus—and himself, he owned—she judged a person not on what rumor whispered, but based on facts and personal observations. She had a heart filled with kindness and a wit that challenged even Lazarus, who had studied at Cambridge. They had welcomed Neville in friendship whenever he happened to be near their home in Stonehall-on-Sea or on Bedford Square, when Lazarus had been transferred to a London church. Before Neville inherited his title, the warmth of the Flanders' house had been a precious haven for him from a life that was often filled with the unexpected.

He could not recall a time since he had met her when she had not been a vital part of his life. Mayhap he had loved her from that first meeting, even though he had never acknowledged those feelings for his best friend's wife. He had thought only that if he ever were want-witted enough to burden himself with a wife, he hoped it would be with someone like Priscilla. That was the only thought he ever allowed to surface, submerging the rest so deeply that he had not been able to retrieve them for months after Lazarus died.

Now he could not imagine why he had hesitated as long as he had to ask her to be his. He grieved the loss of his friend, a void that would always remain in Priscilla's heart as well as his, but he was glad that soon she would share his life and that he would tell her good night before she fell asleep in his arms.

"Is something wrong?" Priscilla asked, brushing at her gown.

"Why do you ask?"

"You are staring at me with the most unusual expression."

He ran his thumb along her cheek and kissed her lightly. To kiss her as he wished would tempt him to sweep her up in his arms and carry her to his bed. To perdition with this boring dinner! He wanted to discover the ecstasy he could share with her.

"Thinking about our life here in the years to come," he said.

Her eyes softened as her fingers swept across his coat. He grasped her elbows and pulled her to him so quickly her hand was pinned between her breasts and his chest. When he captured her mouth, kissing her with the craving that created a hunger nothing in the kitchen could ease, she grasped the top of his waistcoat. Her breath pulsed into his mouth, a heated breeze that heightened the blaze within him.

Even when he heard other voices approaching, it took all his strength to step away from her. Only the thought that her aunt would chide her for being so thoughtless as to kiss him before they sat down to dinner persuaded him to unwrap his arms from around her. Yet he granted himself the pleasure of another swift kiss and watched her eyes close as she savored the enchantment they brought one another.

Neville composed his face as he turned to greet his guests. He was glad he had when he saw Lord Beddlemere walking with the two ladies. Who had invited his neighbor, or had Beddlemere simply decided to give them a look-in? The marquess must be the seventh at the table tonight.

"Interesting," Priscilla said too softly for anyone but him to hear.

"What?"

"You should heed gossip more often, Neville."

"Why? I have heard the tales about myself."

"All gossip is not about you." She smiled. "There has been talk about my aunt's friend and your neighbor."

She carefully spoke no names while Beddlemere, Lady Cordelia, and Lady Barbara laughed at some jest. "This may explain why she is here."

"That is one thing I meant to ask you, Pris. I don't recall her name on the list of guests."

"It was not on it."

"If your aunt—"

"No, she did not invite her friend either. She invited no one, hoping, I suspect, that the evening would be canceled."

He said nothing as Leah ran up to throw her arms around him as if she had not seen him in months. While she chattered about some books she had found at the back of the parlor, he watched Beddlemere and Lady Barbara. Such a match was not out of the question, and the lady must be very serious about her expectations of an offer because she had traveled from Town on the pretense of visiting a friend she could have seen in London or Bath.

Greeting his guests, he motioned for them to take seats at the table. Beddlemere began to speak of the tragic discovery within the mound even before the soup was served. Although Priscilla and her aunt tried to change the subject several times through the courses that followed and Lady Barbara asked questions he knew Priscilla did not want her daughters to hear, the marquess continued to lament about how such a crime could have been committed here.

"Quiet?" Neville asked, realizing the marquess would not be silenced. "Beddlemere, surely you cannot be unaware of the activities along the Cornish shore after the sun sets."

"Smuggling, you mean."

"That, and wrecking."

Beddlemere shook his head and rested his elbows on the table as he pointed at Neville with his fork, much to Lady Cordelia's consternation. "Wreckers have been chased away from the coves north of Padstow. As for smugglers, they exist anywhere in England where the sea and the shore meet." He laughed as he picked up his glass and swirled the wine in it. "Who knows? Mayhap even this excellent vintage arrived in England without the importer paying an excise tax."

"That is possible. From what I have heard, my family has never been afraid of defying the law if they believed it to be in their best interests."

"Is that so? And you, Hathaway?" He lowered his glass, but his face lost none of its intensity. "Are you like the rest of your family?"

"I cannot say." Neville shrugged, closely watching his neighbor's reaction to his apparent indifference. "I have little firsthand knowledge of my family."

Beddlemere smiled. "I see." Turning to Lady Cordelia, he began to talk about a play they both had seen in London.

Priscilla appeared relieved when the subject had changed, and she engaged her daughters in a discussion about a walk along the shore on the morrow. "After Neville and I go into Trepoole," he heard her say, and he was relieved that she intended to join him on the call to Moyle's widow to learn what they could about the dead man.

When Priscilla led the women to look out the windows at the moon-washed sea, Neville regretted not joining them. Beddlemere refilled his glass yet again. Neville had lost count of the number of glasses the marquess had downed, but did not worry because eddlemere's coachman would retrieve him if the marquess drank himself into a stupor.

"Have you heard anything from the constable?" Neville asked.

"Nothing, but I do not expect to," he said in a slurred voice that he was still sober enough to keep hushed, so as not to lure the ladies back to share this conversation. "Kliskey has no head for his position."

"Then he should be replaced."

"By whom? He is the best of the lot in Trepoole."

Neville did not believe that, but arguing the point would be worthless. "Dyson seems to be certain Moyle was often around the excavation."

"Searching for items to pocket and later sell, no doubt." Beddlemere looked at him sternly. "The man met the end he deserved."

"No man deserves to be murdered."

"He was a thief, and, whether he died by someone's hand or at the end of a noose, what does it matter?" Without a pause, he went on, "I must congratulate you, Hathaway. Lady Priscilla should make you a good wife. I understand her son is the current holder of the family's title and is young enough for you to have much influence on him."

"Isaac is Priscilla's son," Neville replied in his coolest tone, "and I would never countermand her decisions about her children."

The marquess chuckled. "But what does a parson's widow know about an earl's upbringing?"

Had Beddlemere been scheming with Lady Cordelia, who had expressed that sentiment far too often? Neville warned himself not to accuse Priscilla's aunt of crimes she very well may not have committed. Lady Cordelia's concerns about Isaac's upbringing—unfounded though they were—might be shared by others in the *ton* who did not know Priscilla well.

"You would be amazed, Beddlemere," he answered.

"On that you are right. I had not guessed a parson's widow would wear a necklace in such a suggestive way." He chuckled before taking a deep drink. "It disappears right at the point where a man's imagination begins."

"Do not be disgusting, Beddlemere. She was not seeking to entice you."

"Not me, most certainly, but you." He laughed. "A wise woman knows she must keep reminding a man what she has to share with him. She may be hoping you are curious enough about what awaits at its end so you fish it out. A most pleasurable fishing expedition for both of you."

Neville wondered if Beddlemere spoke so because he was drunk or if he usually discussed his hostesses so crudely. "She wears her wedding ring on the chain."

"Wedding ring?" He frowned. "I thought you were not yet wed."

"The one given to her by her late husband."

Beddlemere stared at him. "And you allow this?"

"Even if I had a say in the matter—"

"Which you do. As her fiancé, it behooves you to teach Lady Priscilla to meet your expectations before you speak your vows. Teaching a woman afterward is—so I have heard—a far more frustrating exercise because she no longer is as eager to please you in hopes of winning your title and your fortune."

Neville laughed as derisively as Beddlemere had moments before. "First, Priscilla is not a dog to be trained to respond to my commands. Second, she was born with a higher rank than I inherited. Third . . ." He paused. He was not going to discuss the fact that Priscilla would not have cared if he were the wealthiest man in England or a pauper. The love Priscilla offered him was too precious to be spoken of with anyone else, most especially with Beddlemere. "Third, she wears that ring to honor Lazarus's memory. How can I condemn such loyalty?"

"You are a widgeon, Hathaway, to let her rule over you now. She will expect to do the same when you are married."

"Why don't you let me worry about that?"

As he had hoped, Beddlemere's wine-drenched wits gave him no response to such a blunt question. He was glad when the marquess took his leave soon after. Rubbing his forehead, he hoped he would not always get a headache when his neighbor was present. It did not herald happy visits in future to Shadows Fall.

Priscilla closed the door to her daughters' bedchamber. She had been relieved when Mrs. Crosby had told her during dinner that her things would be moved to another room. Although she enjoyed her daughters' company, she was looking forward to having her own private chamber.

She smiled wryly. That was not completely true. She was looking forward to the night when she would be sharing her room with her new husband. His ardent kisses and bewitching touch were a sample of what was to come.

Walking around a corner in the hallway, she gasped when the shadows moved. She laughed shakily. "Neville, you scared a year from my life."

"I hope not. I would not wish to shorten it a second."

"Then stop lurking in the shadows." She wagged a finger at him. "Unless, of course, you are trying to *train* me to be scared of the dark."

"You heard Beddlemere?"

"Yes. He is a beef-head."

"Agreed." He clasped her hand as they continued along the hallway, which was lit by a single lamp. In the dark corridor, if he pulled her into his arms, she was unsure if she could stop herself from surrendering to her longing from him. "I doubt he will be of any help in finding Moyle's murderer."

A chill went through her, banishing her fantasies of his caresses. She could not forget Mr. Moyle's tragic death, but she would have been happy to set it aside for the night.

"I agree," she whispered.

Pausing, he turned her to face him. "Pris, I know how you hate seeing such violence."

"I keep hoping that we will not be caught up in such horrors again." She closed her eyes. "But what bothers me most is that you could be lying dead, too, if you had still been in the east tower."

"I am not, sweetheart." He kissed her brow. "You must stop worrying about what did not happen."

She nodded. His advice was something she should heed. They had a real murder to consider. Thinking about what could have happened and the possibility that the tower's collapse had not been an accident might distract her from uncovering the truth about Gab Moyle's death.

With a lingering kiss good-night, which made her yearn for more, Neville bid her pleasant dreams before continuing along the hallway toward his bedchamber. She did not close her door until she heard his shut at the end of the hall. She smiled as she imagined the time when there would be only a single door to close at the end of the day.

But that was not for tonight. Tonight she needed to sleep well because there was so much to do tomorrow. Not just in preparation for the betrothal ball, but the call on the dead man's widow in the village. Calls on those grieving for a loved one's death were never easy, and when a person had died violently and unexpectedly, the visit was even more difficult. She understood the need to appear composed during the crisis. She also understood it was a sham, for she had struggled with those uneven emotions after Lazarus died. She had wanted to seem strong for the children and the rest of the family as well as their friends. Doing what needed to be done and comforting those around her had made her feel like a machine repeating the same tasks without thought or sentiment.

She only hoped that tomorrow she could show Mrs. Moyle how such good intentions led to a very private perdition. The widow might not have a dear friend, like Neville, to help her through the worst.

Sighing, Priscilla pushed away from the door. The chamber where she would be sleeping tonight was smaller than the one she had shared with her daughters last night. The window offered a grand view of the sea, which was ink dark beneath the stars. She wondered when the moon had set. She stared at the spot where water washed up on the shore. The sea concealed its secrets well, but had released some pieces to puzzle her.

Nobody had given her an answer earlier to her question about how the flagon found on the shore could have reached the beach unbroken. So many rocks were scattered along the beach, and larger ones, ringed by foam, farther out in the water. Mayhap the sea had washed away part of the cliff during a recent storm. That could have revealed the flagon. Mr. Randall had spoken of his belief that the village surrounding the temple might have been extensive.

Walking away from the window, she explored the rest of the cramped room. The hearth was blackened with smoke from the centuries it had warmed this room. A table next to the bed balanced on three legs against the wall. She would have to find a better table if she wanted to do any correspondence here. Her nightgown and wrapper stretched across the narrow bed.

She heard a low chirp and looked up at the rafters crisscrossing the ceiling. There must be a bird's nest hidden there. She would have it removed in the morning, but tonight she was appreciative of any company.

She readied herself for bed, missing her daughters' chatter. Her abigail, Glenda, had a bed in the rooms where the rest of the household staff slept, because there was no room or bed for Glenda. As soon as possible, other arrangements must be made.

Sitting on the bed, she settled the coverlet over her shoulders. Damp scents left from their days on the road drifted out of the fabric as she leaned back against the simple headboard and stared out the window. Dust distorted the starlight. Getting the panes cleaned in the bedchambers would be a priority tomorrow.

So much to do, and it all needed to be done before the betrothal ball. She was glad Aunt Cordelia was here to help oversee the work. That would free her to help Neville uncover any clues about what had happened in the temple mound.

But she could not think of that before she went to sleep. If she did, she would start thinking about that accursed tower again. She wished Neville was right, but she feared he was wrong

SEVEN

Priscilla?

The voice broke through Priscilla's dream. Raising her head, she blinked as she tried to look through the darkness. Who was calling to her in the middle of the night? It was not her daughters or her aunt.

Priscilla?

It was a man's voice.

"Neville?" she murmured. Having him in her room would create all sorts of problems. But it could not be Neville. No matter how much they longed to be together, he would do nothing to compromise her reputation.

Priscilla?

All words were lost behind the fear clogging her throat as a strange light appeared where there had been none only a heartbeat ago. The colorless light grew in the corner beyond the door. She stared, her hands clutching the coverlet.

Priscilla?

She shuddered as the voice resonated through her head.

Priscilla?

No, it could not be! She must be imagining it. She stared at the light. Her stomach cramped. Something was assuming shape within it. She wanted to call for help. To call for Neville, so he could assure her that she was imagining all this.

Her voice stuck in her throat.

Priscilla, listen to me. Priscilla?

The light shifted and contorted like a beast in agony. Something began to ooze from within it. Something . . . She screamed as a disembodied arm reached out of the light toward her.

It had to be a bad dream! It could not be real. Then something touched her. A hand? With a shriek, she jumped out of bed. Her left ankle twisted beneath her. She moaned, but rushed to the door, groping frantically for the latch. She could not find it.

She risked a glance over her shoulder. The light roiled and eddied like a turbulent storm. Who was there? Someone real or a phantom? When fingers emerged from the light again, she ripped open the door and threw herself into the dusky passage.

She choked as she hit something as hard as the stone walls. Her breath exploded from her as arms imprisoned her. She tried to squirm away. She had to get away. If that—that *thing* touched her . . .

"Pris, what is wrong?"

She raised her head and stared up into dark eyes wide with shock. "Neville!"

"What is it? Did I hear you scream?"

She flung her arms around him. If her aunt or Lady Barbara chanced to see her dressed in her nightgown and in Neville's arms, there would be the devil to pay. She did not care. She wanted to be safe in his loving arms. Pressing her face to his linen shirt, she slid her hands up his muscular back. She heard his heart falter for a single beat, then race to the speed of hers.

He tilted her head back, and she stared into his eyes again. His fingers grazed her cheek as gently as the first, enticing spring breeze. Not even the shadows could conceal the glitter of longing in his eyes. Coal dark and tempting, his gaze invited her to lose herself within them. Her fingers ran through his ebony hair and curved along his neck. Her breasts brushed his chest, sending pleasure swirling deep within her as she tilted his mouth toward hers. She ached for the warmth of his breath upon her lips to wash away the icy terror.

His gaze held hers as his face lowered. Splaying his fingers across her back, he brought her even closer. She held her breath, not wanting even a slight sound to ruin this enchanted moment.

A moan came from her room, and Priscilla whirled to stare at the open door in horror. The glow from within diminished and vanished.

"What is going on?" Neville tried to concentrate on what Priscilla was saying, but it was difficult. He wanted to think about her in his arms with nothing but the finest linen between her and his fingertips. Her golden hair, falling about her shoulders, teased him to bury his face in it. His heart thudded as he fought the craving to tug her back into his arms. She had offered her lips to him, and he wanted to taste them.

When she wobbled, he gripped her elbow. Her hand covered his, gripping it with desperation. Her face was as colorless as the foam breaking on the waves.

"I don't know what is going on." She took a single step, then winced.

"You screamed."

"Don't remind me that I sounded like a coward. I was half asleep, and—"

He stroked her hand. "It is all right, Pris. You do not

need to be brave all the time. Even I, although I would deny it most vigorously to anyone else, have been frightened."

She did not smile. "Is it still there?"

"It?"

She pointed toward her bedroom. "A bright glow surrounded whatever it was."

He stepped into her room. When he saw no hint of light, he frowned. "There is nothing here."

"I saw something."

"What?"

She hesitated, then whispered, "It looked like a ghost."

"Pris—"

"Don't tell me how stupid it is to say I saw a ghost, but I am not sure what else to call it." She explained what she had seen.

Neville chuckled humorlessly. "That describes what I would say was a ghost."

"I should dress you down for giving me a haunted bedroom." She took a single step, then gasped. "I twisted my ankle. It hurts."

"Let me help you."

He held out his hand. She hesitated. Because she was unsure what might be in the room? No, Priscilla would never be so overmastered by a ghostly intruder that she would falter. It must be— He saw her glance down the hall, and he knew she was making sure her aunt was not nearby. He wanted to commend her good sense in averting any extra trouble. At the same time, he needed to chide her for being so foolish. She was hurt. Even propriety must be set aside at times.

She put her fingers on his palm. He said nothing as

she tried to take a single step. Pain dug into her face. "I cannot."

"Then I will help you."

He lifted her carefully. Pulling her against his chest, he drew in the scent of her flowery perfume. Her soft curves molded perfectly to him. When her arm settled around his shoulder, her hair brushed across his chin in a dozen separate caresses.

Crossing the narrow room, he settled her on the bed and draped the coverlet over her. "Pris, you should have your ankle strapped."

"Forget that!"

"You could injure yourself worse if—"

She rose to her knees and clutched his sleeves. "It was between the window and the door. It—" She shuddered. "It touched me."

"It touched you?" He fought to constrain his fury. Someone pretending to be a phantom to frighten her was outrageous, but to be so bold was a greater crime. Putting his hands on her shoulders, he pushed her down amid the pillows and leaned over her. "Now explain what—"

"What is going on here?" came an appalled voice from behind him.

Neville did not want to turn around, but he did. Lady Cordelia stood in the doorway. Behind her, Daphne and Leah were both wide-eyed and giggling. As if it were commonplace to find him beside Priscilla's bed, he said, "That is what I had hoped to discover."

"With my niece?" Lady Cordelia strode toward him, her half-buttoned wrapper flapping behind her. "You may be her fiancé"—her glower revealed that she still hoped Priscilla would come to her senses and change her mind about marrying him—"but that does not afford you *carte blanche* to be in her room."

"But a ghost does."

"A ghost?" asked the lady and Leah at the same time.

Leah bounced on her mother's bed. "You saw a ghost, Mama? A real ghost?"

"Real and ghost are not two words you should use in the same sentence," Priscilla said, her voice revealing no sign of her distress of moments ago.

Neville left her to explain to her daughters and aunt as he examined the room. Even when he lit the lamp, he could see no signs of what had created the illusion of a spectral visitor. Nothing was hidden in a corner or by the window. He waited for Lady Cordelia to leave, so he could speak to Priscilla about what he had not found. He almost laughed at his own air-dreaming. Priscilla's aunt would not leave until he did, fearing he would cross the bounds of propery.

Knowing that Lady Cordelia would strain to hear every word he spoke, he kissed Priscilla on the forehead. He shook his head, and Priscilla nodded with understanding. Her eyes remained troubled when she looked past him. He could read her thoughts as if they were his own . . . because they were.

It could not have been a ghost she had seen, but she had seen something. The question was what.

The village of Trepoole consisted of a pair of shops, a church, and two terraces of cottages along a straggling street. A few detached cottages were scattered on the road between the center of the village and the sea cliffs. Sheep dotted the fields on the far side of the hedgerows growing close to the narrow track running inland from the sea.

Fishing boats in the harbor were hung with lanterns that had been lit against the morning fog. Flickering lights danced with the motion of the waves, splashing light into ever-changing pools. More lamps shone through the houses' windows. For hundreds of years, Trepoole had stood here, slowly embracing the changes of time, but only on its own terms.

In spite of the twinges in her left ankle, Priscilla was glad the carriage had been left at Shadows Fall. Driving along the narrow street would have drawn everyone's attention to her and Neville, as well as to their destination. Mayhap it had not mattered whether they drove or walked. She saw doors open in their wake and faces appearing in windows. More than one matron seemed to have chosen this exact moment to come out and sweep her front steps. Although this small town was on the opposite side of England, she suspected it was much like Stonehall-on-Sea, where nothing went unnoted.

She glanced toward the small, square church with its thick tower. Seeking the assistance of the local pastor might be necessary if Mrs. Moyle was unwilling to speak to them. She blinked back tears. The moment of discovering that a husband would never return was shattering, and she did not want to imagine how it would be to learn that a spouse had been murdered.

"Pris," Neville said quietly, "I know how difficult this is for you."

"It is." She would not dissemble with him. Since they had passed by the double wooden gates in the wall between Shadows Fall and the road leading into Trepoole, she had dreaded this call on Mrs. Moyle more with every step. "Yet I may be able to help her because I understand her grief and I understand how little I understand."

He smiled. "That may be the most confusing thing you have ever said to me."

"Because I am unsettled."

He patted her hand on his arm. "If you would prefer not to continue—"

"Do not coddle me, Neville."

"I was not intending to. I just wanted to be sure you wanted to do this *today*."

"If you are talking about my foolishness last night with that apparent ghost, you need not worry."

"But I am." His jaw worked as his lips straightened. "Someone was in your bedroom last night. That concerns me a great deal."

"As it does me."

"I will have Mrs. Crosby move you to another room tonight."

Priscilla shook her head. "Do not make more work for that poor woman. She has too much to do now with trying to get Shadows Fall ready in time for the ball." Giving him a smile, she added, "Mayhap my ghost was simply lost because it had haunted the tower which is not there any longer."

"That is absurd."

"Everything about that tower is absurd."

When he did not argue, she glanced at him. He wore the expression that displayed his fury. At whom? At the murderer? At her for believing the fall of the tower could have been aimed at hurting or killing him? At whoever had created the ghost? She still was vexed with herself for reacting with such terror. If it had not awakened her with that whisper and then touched her . . . She shivered. She needed to stop thinking about that and focus on helping Mrs. Moyle and getting some information about the dead man.

Priscilla stopped in front of the Moyles' cottage. She walked across the stones that were pressed into the earth in the front garden and up to the door. When Neville remained silent, she rapped on the door.

It opened, and a woman with light brown hair peeked out. Her gown was simple and covered by an apron dusted with flour. Her mobcap had a flamboyant ruffle which shadowed her face. Priscilla could see the remnants of tears on her cheeks.

"Yes?" asked the woman in a thick Cornish accent.

"I am Priscilla Flanders, and this is Sir Neville Hathaway."

"Of Shadows Fall?"

"Yes. May we come in?"

The woman nodded and stepped aside. When she gestured, the light glinted off a ring on her left forefinger. It looked like the ring her husband had been wearing when they found his body.

With a glance at Neville, Priscilla stepped into the small cottage. It was cramped with a ceiling so low that Neville had to duck to avoid the rafters, but the stone floor and the wooden table and benches were clean. A bed was pushed up against the wall beside the hearth. Several pallets were shoved beneath it, and she remembered that the Moyles had a large family.

"Please sit down," Mrs. Moyle said. "May I offer you some tea?"

Neville started to demur, but Priscilla hurried to say, "Thank you, Mrs. Moyle." She had learned as a pastor's wife that even the poorest family had a sense of pride that should be acknowledged by accepting their hospitality. As she sat on the closest bench, she added, "I hope you will accept my sympathies on your husband's death."

Mrs. Moyle halted as she was reaching for the tea kettle. Her sob was quickly hushed when she poured water into a dark brown china teapot. Bringing it to the table, she said, "That is very kind of you to say, my lady."

"We want you to know that we intend to ensure that everything possible is done to find his murderer," Neville said.

She flinched, but nodded. "Thank you, Sir Neville. It is very kind of you to say that, too."

Priscilla saw Neville's dismay, and she knew he regretted saying *murderer.* She could assure him—and Mrs. Moyle—that he had not intended to distress the widow more by speaking plainly, but that was sure to make the situation more strained. Instead, she asked Mrs. Moyle about her children and how they fared. The dead man's children now would be dependent on charity. When Mrs. Moyle spoke of her extended family around Trepoole, Priscilla was somewhat relieved.

"What sort of man was your late husband?" she asked while Mrs. Moyle poured pale tea for them.

"A good man. Gab worked hard."

"That is what we have heard." Priscilla took a sip of the weak tea. "Was he a fisherman?"

"He fished when he could get a job on one of the boats."

"And other times?"

"He always did what he could to keep his children from starving."

"Mrs. Moyle, your husband sounds like a fine man."

"He was."

"May I ask about the ring you are wearing? He was wearing one as well."

Mrs. Moyle ran her finger along the ring. "He gave me this when we were hand-fasted the year before we wed in the church. He made them himself during the summer he worked in the tin mines. Lots of the men used to work in the mines when the fishing was bad." She looked down at her ring. "He made one for me and one for himself."

"What is the symbol on it?"

"I think it was the first letter in his name." Her wan face filled with color for a moment, embarrassed to own that she could not read.

"May I look more closely at it?"

When Mrs. Moyle held out her hand, Priscilla realized the widow could not take off the ring. Her fingers must have widened with the passage of years. The ring was crudely made, and the symbol on it had almost been worn down into oblivion. It might have been the letter *G*, but Priscilla could not be certain.

Neville cleared his throat, and Priscilla glanced at him again. He had to ask questions that would be harder for Mrs. Moyle to answer.

"Do you know of any enemies your husband might have had?" he asked. "Someone who wished him harm?"

"Enemies?" Mrs. Moyle rose and went back to the hearth. "Gab had no enemies, sir. He was a kindhearted man who thought only of his family." Her shoulders shook as she hid her face in her apron.

Neville looked at Priscilla. She came to her feet and put her hand on his shoulder. They had pushed too hard because Mrs. Moyle was becoming overwrought with her grief. Yet it was necessary if they were to discover who had killed Gab Moyle.

Going over to Mrs. Moyle, Priscilla said, "Excuse Sir Neville for asking that. He wishes only to help."

"I know," she whispered from behind her apron.

"If you have not yet been told by the constable, Professor Dyson—"

"The man digging in the dirt?"

"Yes." She dampened her arid lips before saying, "He has accused your husband of stealing from him."

"Gab would not do that." Mrs. Moyle's shoulders shook as another sob filtered through her apron. "He said the professor was beef-headed to spend his days in the dirt. He said nobody ever found anything of value digging in an empty field."

Priscilla glanced at Neville. That Gab Moyle had spoken of the excavation at all suggested he had interest in it. Searching the house to see if they could uncover a stolen relic would be silly. Not only would that disturb his widow more, but Priscilla doubted Mr. Moyle would hide anything of value in the house, which would be the first place the constable would investigate.

"It is rumored that many break the King's laws along these shores," Priscilla said. "Could your husband have angered one of them?"

"The smugglers?" The apron dropped away from her face as she stared at Priscilla in horror. "Do not even hint at such things, my lady. Gab was smart enough to stay away from *them*. Everyone in Trepoole knows what happens if someone crosses *them*."

"They are killed?" asked Neville from near the table.

Mrs. Moyle looked at him, her face ashen. "Mayhap."

"Mayhap?"

"No one knows what truly happens, sir. If someone crosses *them*, that person disappears. Dead? Mayhap, but who can know for sure?" She looked out the window toward the sea. "They just vanish forever."

Neville was glad Priscilla suggested another stop before they left Trepoole. She was shaken by Mrs. Moyle's words about the smugglers. In spite of everything she had experienced, Priscilla was gentle at heart. She could contend with evil when she encountered it, but some wickedness she was unable to imagine.

Neville could. There was a great deal of profit to be made from smuggling goods ashore and avoiding the excise men. Those involved would not want to lose a farthing, and they would go to great lengths to make sure anyone trying to halt them failed. But how did they make it appear as if someone evaporated into the morning mist? A body would eventually be found in the fields around the village. Mayhap it was time to explore some of the seaside caves.

"Let's call here," Priscilla said, her soft voice gliding through his thoughts as easily as she slipped into his arms.

He realized they were standing in front of what must be the vicar's house, because it was set beside the church. Nodding, he went with her to the simple stone cottage.

The vicar, whom he knew was named Reverend Mr. Rosewarne, answered the door. His spectacles caught the sunlight. He lifted them off to reveal kindly brown eyes. "Good day. How may I help you?"

"I am Priscilla Flanders," Priscilla said with a smile.

"How can I help you, Miss—Mrs.—?"

"Lady Priscilla," Neville supplied quietly.

The vicar's eyes widened. "*Lady* Priscilla, how may I help you?"

"Sir Neville Hathaway—"

"Hathaway? Of Shadows Fall?" His eyes widened even further.

"Yes, Vicar."

"Come in." He opened the door and ushered them into a comfortable room. It was overfilled with a pair of settees and a large desk. With the three of them, there was barely enough room for him to close the door behind them.

When he motioned toward the settees, Priscilla sat on one. Neville perched next to her, and he realized he had been betwattled by the tiny room. The settee was so short his knees rose almost to his chin.

"How may I help you?" asked the parson.

"We have come from calling on Mrs. Moyle," Neville said.

"Such a tragedy."

"Yes, but it will be a greater tragedy if Moyle's killer is not brought to justice."

"On that we agree." He picked up a pipe from the table beside his chair and lit it. "You should know, Sir Neville, that Constable Kliskey has been thwarted in his investigation of this horrible crime."

"Already?" Priscilla asked.

The vicar's brows lowered. "I do not understand your question, my lady."

"The body was discovered only yesterday. How can the constable believe there is nothing else he can do when so little time has passed?"

"You misunderstand me. I said he was thwarted, and he is, because no one in Trepoole is eager to be seen speaking to him."

Neville nodded. The smugglers held this village in a death grip, threatening anyone who endangered their work with a quick passing. Quick? He could not be certain of that, but he suspected he was right. The smugglers would not chance being seen while they dispatched their victims. Or, he reminded himself, nobody was brave enough to watch the shore in hopes of saving someone at the risk of his or her own life.

"Do you have any idea who leads the smugglers?" Neville asked.

"You should know the answer to that question better than I."

"Why?"

Reverend Mr. Rosewarne rubbed his hand against his thigh as his fingers tightened on his pipe. "Oh, that is right. I forgot you have had little to do with your family's past. You had a life of your own in the theater before you inherited the title and the lands here near Trepoole."

"You seem to know quite a bit about Neville," Priscilla said.

"It is spoken of openly in the village."

"So we had guessed." She gave him a warm smile. "My late husband was a vicar as well. He was privy to many of the rumors that filled his parish."

The vicar smiled back, and Neville wondered if anyone could resist Priscilla's warmth. "I am glad you realize, my lady, that there is nothing malicious in the gossip."

"Just curiosity."

Neville slanted forward, resting his elbows on his knees. "And I am curious about your comments that *I* should know the smugglers' leader."

"The Hathaways have, in the past, been deeply involved with all parts of life here in Cornwall." Reverend Mr. Rosewarne puffed on his pipe, sending smoke curling around his head.

Priscilla laughed. "It would appear, Neville, your family has a long history of doing exactly as they wish, whether it is completely legal or not."

"Yes," added the vicar. "The Hathaways came here with the dissolution of the monasteries and purchased the lands belonging to Shadows Fall. It is said that the grand house standing there now cost far more than the baronet of the time had planned."

"So he turned to other sources of income?" Neville smiled. "Smuggling and wrecking and, I assume, an occasional raid on his neighbors."

"There are stories of a full herd of sheep being stolen as well as an accusation—never proved—that some of the younger sons enjoyed escapades along the roads. A few of their victims described the hooded highwaymen so perfectly that nobody doubted they were from Shadows Fall, but not one was brought before the justice of the peace."

"But that is in the past. Who leads the smugglers now?"

He put down his pipe. "I wish I could tell you. I have asked that question many times myself, but each person I ask claims ignorance. Even the men I know are involved profess not to know."

While the vicar changed the subject to Priscilla's arrival at Shadows Fall and how she liked Cornwall and how long she and her family were staying and wasn't it wonderful that the house was being lived in again, Neville pondered what Reverend Mr. Rosewarne had told him. That his family had made their fortune with illicit activities was a rather intriguing idea that fit with everything else he had ever heard about his ancestors. Yet the stories offered no clue as to who had taken advantage of an absent Hathaway to assume control of the smugglers. That was something he intended to find out posthaste.

He said as much to Priscilla when they left the village behind and were walking back to Shadows Fall.

She stared out at where Professor Dyson and his assistant were digging near the mound. "I had hoped you would see the wisdom of leaving that aspect to the authorities."

"Kliskey?" He snorted. "The man seems barely able to find his way home. How can one expect him to find such information?"

"I assume you have a plan on how to obtain this information."

"Of course."

"Do you intend to share your plan, or will you be as closemouthed as the villagers?"

He paused, putting his foot on a stile beside the road. "It is simple, Pris, so simple I am astonished you have to ask."

"Did you consider I was trying to make you explain so you would see the lunacy of whatever you plan?"

"Lunacy? How do you know it is not a brilliant plan?"

She arched a brow at him, mocking the motion he had made often.

"It *is* a brilliant plan, Pris, and a simple one. I intend to assert my ancestral rights."

She stared and gasped, "You cannot be serious!"

"Quite serious. I intend to take my place as leader of the smugglers."

EIGHT

The sun rose out of the agitated sea and a cold breeze came off the water as Priscilla walked along the cliffs. The storm that stirred up the waves must have passed beyond Land's End, for she had not heard any rain last night, and she had been awake all night. If she mentioned that to anyone else at Shadows Fall, they would have assumed she wanted to avoid another encounter with that ghost—or whatever it was. That was true, but thinking the ghost would return was not what had kept her from sleeping.

How could Neville be so shortsighted? It was unlike him to act out of hand, because he usually considered every facet of an action before he embarked on it. She had seen no signs of that with his ploy to assume his family's role as the leaders of the smugglers. Although she had to own such a plan could lead to the discovery of who terrorized the villagers, it also could be far more dangerous than anything she had ever known him to do.

"But there may be so many things you know nothing of," she said aloud, hoping the sound of her voice would bring some comfort. Had Neville been in such jeopardy before? Mayhap he had, but that changed nothing.

She looked at the house perched on the cliff. Dawn

gilded the windows, and if anyone else was awake, she saw no sign. Mayhap Neville had found sleep easier than she had. The sleep of the innocent? She wanted to laugh, but her spirits were too grim. Neville Hathaway was about as far from innocent as was humanly possible.

She heard the click of metal on stone and looked down to see Mr. Randall digging at the base of the cliff. Professor Dyson was examining something between two of the larger boulders. Did they hope to find more artifacts like the flagon? She wished them good luck, but would be amazed if they were so fortunate.

Should she and Neville have searched the shore for information about the smugglers? Any clues there were now obliterated by Professor Dyson's explorations. Looking to her left, she shaded her eyes so she could see what might be caves or just a hollow in the cliff walls.

She picked up a small stone that had been rounded by the sand and water. Bouncing it in her hand, she sighed. Too many questions and no answers.

"Good morning."

Priscilla glanced over her shoulder to see her older daughter walking around a boulder. Daphne held her lacy parasol over the top of her straw bonnet, but beneath her spencer she wore a gown that she would not take with her when they returned to London for her first Season and the wedding. It was well worn and would not be harmed further by walking through the fields.

"Good morning," Priscilla replied, trying not to let her frustration fill her voice.

"You are up early, Mama."

"I enjoy early mornings by the sea."

"Even when it is chilly?" She shivered.

Motioning for her daughter to sit beside her on the boulder, she smiled. "*You* are up early, and I know you do not share my interest in a morning walk along the shore."

"I had a hard time getting to sleep last night."

"If you are worried about what has been happening—"

"I try not to think of that poor dead man."

Priscilla nodded. "Good, for you should trust the constable to handle the matter."

"No, I trust you and Uncle Neville to find out the truth. You know how to do that." She shivered as she looked toward the mound.

"Then what is disturbing you so much you cannot sleep?"

Daphne's voice rose. "Mama, Aunt Cordelia has said I must not attend the whole ball because I am not yet launched on the Season." She lowered her parasol. "How can I not attend when you announce your betrothal?"

She put her arm around her daughter's shoulders. "Your great-aunt is very concerned about you making the very, very best impression when you are fired off. You should appreciate her anxiety on your behalf."

"I have tried to be appreciative."

"Good, and do not brood about the ball. While you will not be able to attend all of it—" She held up her hand to halt her daughter's protests. "While you will not be able to attend all of the evening's activities, you and your sister will be able to participate in ways you may not have thought about."

"What ways?"

Priscilla smiled. "You must let me speak with Neville before I make any promises."

"You are letting Uncle Neville tell you what to do?"

"If so, that will be a first," said Neville as he clambered over the boulder to sit next to Daphne. "Your mother has never been one to distrust her own instincts. Good morning, Pris." His kiss was a mere wisp of sensation across her lips, even though his eyes blazed with the yearning for the kiss he would have given her if Daphne had not been watching. "What are you doing out here at dawn, Pris?"

"Did you consider that I was trying to find someplace to be alone with my thoughts?" she replied.

"No, for this lovely young woman is already keeping you company." He winked at Daphne, who giggled. All signs of the recent infatuation she had had for him had vanished, and once more they treated each other with the warmth of a young girl and a beloved uncle. "Am I intruding on some discussion that should be shared only by mothers and daughters?"

Daphne stood. "I will leave you to talk to Uncle Neville, Mama."

Neville watched Daphne walk back toward the house before saying, "That sounds ominous."

"Just Daphne who can barely endure waiting until she is a part of the *ton*." Priscilla smiled.

"I will leave such matters to you."

"The children will be your responsibility, too, when we are married."

He laughed. "I will gladly teach Isaac what I can, but your daughters? I am quite helpless in that quarter, for I know nothing about females."

"Really?" She stroked his cheek. "I would say you know quite a bit about women, Neville Hathaway."

"Do not judge by present company. You are an extraordinary woman, as I believe I have mentioned once or twice in the past. To what other woman could I suggest a walk along the shore and she would understand I had ulterior motives that had, unfortunately, nothing to do with her?" He stood and held out his hand. "Shall we, Pris?"

"I think that is a good idea." She let him bring her to her feet.

As he drew her hand into his arm, he smiled. "This is an exception, I want you to know. Usually my ulterior motives are focused on you."

"So I have seen." Priscilla walked with him along the path, which was so narrow he trod through the high grass at its edge. "What is your ulterior motive this morning?"

"To see what I might discover of smuggling activity in this cove."

"Do you think the owls leave signs to point to their hideaways?"

He laughed. "That would be too easy."

"Is there anything I can say to make you reconsider your jobbernowl plan to challenge the smugglers' leader?"

"No."

She waited for him to add more, but he said nothing other than to take care as he turned onto a steep path leading down the cliff's face. When Neville was taciturn, it could mean only one thing. He believed she was safer not knowing what he intended to do next. Bother!

Halfway down the cliff, Priscilla saw a motion farther along the beach. She shaded her eyes again so she could better see two people strolling toward where the men were working among the stones. "It appears the professor and Mr. Randall are about to have company."

"Interesting." He squinted into the sun. "Lord Beddlemere, I would guess, but who is with him?"

"Lady Barbara."

"Interesting," he said again as they continued down

the cliff to its base. "Before your comments when Beddlemere came to dinner, I was not aware they were acquainted."

"Aunt Cordelia will know any details."

His eyes took on a decidedly roguish twinkle. "Who would have guessed I would be dependent on your aunt for the latest *on dits?*"

"I would have, because she knows what is happening with the Polite World before even those involved know."

"She did not guess you would say yes when I asked you most sincerely to be my wife."

Priscilla was unsure what she would have replied, but it did not matter. Professor Dyson took note of them and rushed over with an enthusiastic greeting.

"I trust your generosity in allowing us to explore your estate includes the shore," he said to Neville.

"You are welcome to look about wherever you wish, but if you are planning to dig up the floors of the house, please be courteous enough to inform me first so I do not walk over you."

"Yes, yes." The flustered professor looked at Priscilla in an obvious plea to help him know how to react to Neville's hoaxing.

She was tempted to tell him to take the comments at face value and respond appropriately, but asked, "Have you had any luck in finding anything here?"

"Yes."

"Yes?" Her voice squeaked with astonishment.

"Something else survived being in the sea?" Neville's face revealed only faint curiosity, but Priscilla knew he was as shocked as she was.

"Amazing, isn't it?" The professor turned. "Randall, bring over that cup you—we found."

Neville smiled at the professor taking credit for his assistant's work, but his expression returned to mild interest when Professor Dyson looked at him and began chattering about what an important site this was proving to be.

Priscilla watched Mr. Randall walk toward them with care. He held his hands together as if carrying water. When he reached them, he glanced from her to Neville. At the slightest nod from Neville, he handed the cup to Priscilla.

She balanced the cup on her palm. It was wide and shallow and had once had two handles. Neither remained, and the base was broken in half. The edges were chipped, but the delicate red painting on the black glaze outlined human figures growing grapes and making wine. It was lovely.

"Do you think this came from the temple?" she asked.

Mr. Randall opened his mouth to reply, but the professor interjected, "Where else would such a fine piece be used? Ah, Lord Beddlemere, come and see what we have discovered this morning."

The marquess boomed a greeting, then asked, "What do you have there, my lady?"

"A cup that was discovered just a short time ago." She balanced the cup with care as Lord Beddlemere looked over her right shoulder and Lady Barbara around her left one. "It is quite amazing."

"It is beyond amazing." He lifted the cup from her hand and held it with great care. "Look at the colors and the carving on it."

The professor grinned. "It was made by a master."

"A master with the rarest of talents." Lord Beddlemere gazed at the cup with an obvious desire to own it.

She had not guessed he would be so interested in an artifact, for he had paid no attention to the wonderful temple within the mound. But he had, she recalled, been fascinated with the flagon found on the beach. He had still been holding it when she and Neville left the mound. She wondered where it was now.

"It is unbelievable," he continued, "that it has survived this long at the bottom of the sea."

Priscilla watched Mr. Randall's face while Lord Beddlemere continued to exclaim over the cup. He was struggling to smile, but the despair dimming his eyes told her he considered the cup's survival unbelievable as well. She stepped aside and motioned to Mr. Randall. He followed her a short distance along the stony shore, and she guessed he was anxious to reveal to someone why the cup was upsetting him.

"The cup could not have come from the temple." The words burst from him as soon as they were out of earshot of the others.

That statement was not what she had expected him to say. "Was it commonly used in a household?"

"Yes, but not at this site."

She frowned. "I do not understand what you mean, Mr. Randall."

"The cup is not Roman."

"If it was made by a local artisan—"

"My lady, the cup is Greek."

"Greek?" She looked at where Lady Barbara was holding the cup as Professor Dyson pointed to something on it. "Certainly it could have been brought here by someone who settled along the coast."

"It could have been."

"You sound as if you truly doubt that."

He nodded. "I do, my lady, because the cup bears no signs of having been in the sea for centuries."

"Are you suggesting someone left it here on the shore for you to find?"

"Possibly, or it may not have been intentional. It could have been dropped without being noticed."

"In the middle of the night?" she asked, choosing her words with care. "By someone who was in a great hurry and did not want to be seen?"

Mr. Randall glanced around them before whispering, "It is possible."

She looked at Neville, who was still deep in discussion with the others. What would he have to say about this new puzzle?

Constable Kliskey looked up when the tavern door opened. When he saw who stood in the doorway, he hastily tilted back his ale. He needed some fortifying if Sir Neville Hathaway started firing questions at him again. The baronet had come into Trepoole shortly after midday, seeking him. So many questions, and the man had expected him to have an answer to all of them.

Even if he had information about the smugglers who prowled through the cove near Shadows Fall, he would be cursed before he spoke of it to Hathaway. He would be doubly cursed if he opened his mouth and the smugglers discovered he was prattling like an old woman. Everyone knew what had happened to that excise officer from Padstow. Even though the officer had been warned, he had continued to stick his nose into business best ignored. He had vanished, just like anyone else who tried to find out about the smugglers.

Letting Hathaway continue to probe into matters in Trepoole could mean the baronet disappearing, too. That would create a hullabaloo like the village had never seen. Someone—mayhap his fiancée—would be sure to demand an investigation. What had placated Moyle's wife would not soothe Lady Priscilla. Would the smugglers slay an earl's mother? He no longer could be certain what they would do.

That was why he stayed at the tavern on most nights. If something happened, he would have witnesses who could swear he was not involved.

He frowned when Hathaway lurched toward where a keg of ale waited. Was the baronet already in his cups? That could explain why Hathaway was here instead of at that hulking ruin by the sea cliffs.

Hathaway pounded his fist on the counter by the keg, and every eye in the tavern focused on him. Tremeer, the tavernkeeper, got up from his seat by the hearth and rushed to where the baronet stood.

"Can I help you, Sir Neville?" Tremeer asked, his balding pate glistening with sweat. If the man sat any closer to the fire, he would have had to perch on the embers.

"Is this everyone?" The baronet's words were slurred.

"Everyone?"

"Everyone in Trepoole."

Kliskey lifted his glass again as Tremeer looked in his direction. The baronet was the tavernkeeper's problem, not his.

"I don't understand," Tremeer said, wringing his hands in his apron. Was he thinking of the last Hathaways who had spent time at Shadows Fall?

That one had been a lout whose main interest focused on asserting his rights as lord of the manor upon any maiden he chanced to encounter. No one knew how many bastards he had sired around Trepoole. Another Hathaway had had the grand idea of mining in an area where the ground was unstable. Fortunately he had killed himself before anyone else died. What strange ideas would the current Hathaway have to inflict on Trepoole?

Hathaway swore vividly. "There is nothing to understand. I asked only if everyone in Trepoole was here."

Kliskey took another hasty drink as the tavernkeeper again looked at him. He swallowed only air. His mug was empty, but Tremeer could not see that from where he stood.

"The women and children—"

The baronet's oath silenced Tremeer. "Who in perdition cares about what women and sniveling brats are doing? Is every man in Trepoole here?"

Kliskey glanced around the tavern and was surprised to see that every man was. Even the vicar was sitting near the door, a cup of tea in front of him. The vicar caught his eye, and Kliskey tipped back his empty glass again.

"They all are here, Sir Neville." Tremeer looked ready to wring his hands right through his apron's thick fabric. "Is there anything we can do for you?"

Hathaway motioned toward the keg, and the tavernkeeper quickly filled a mug for him. Taking a deep drink, Hathaway wiped the back of his hand across his mouth. He set the mug on the counter.

"For any of you who do not know, I am Sir Neville Hathaway of Shadows Fall."

No one moved or spoke.

"My family has long been away from Shadows Fall."

Kliskey thought he heard someone say, "Thank goodness." He could not be certain. It may have only been his own thoughts.

"But *I* am here now, and it is my intention to assume

the responsibilities and duties that belong to my family."
Hathaway hiccupped. Downing more ale, he went on,
his voice growing stronger on every word. "*All* the duties that belong to my family. If anyone wishes to gainsay
me on this, speak up now."

The constable gasped when the vicar stood. Was he
out of his mind?

"There are some duties that should remain unful-
filled," Reverend Mr. Rosewarne said with quiet dignity.
"Too many men from Trepoole have died to put gold
into the purses of the Hathaway family."

"And in their own pockets as well," Hathaway fired
back. "I am looking for men who are willing to abide by
their obligations, too. The rights to everything that
washes ashore in the cove belong to Shadows Fall."

"Is that why you came to Trepoole?" asked the vicar
as the other men listened intently.

"Why else would I be here?"

"I heard you are planning some sort of fancy gathering there."

"Such a distance from London?" Hathaway laughed.
"Who would believe the *ton* would come to Cornwall to
attend a betrothal ball when the Season is getting underway in London?"

The men glanced at each other and nodded. Kliskey
wondered why he had not considered this before now.

"A betrothal ball," the baronet went on, "is the perfect cloak for my intention to assert my manorial
rights." Motioning to the tavernkeeper, he called, "Another round for my friends." He smiled. "I am looking
for men who would be interested in steady work. All
profit will be divided among the men participating. I
get two shares. Every other man gets a single share."

Kliskey was not the only one to gasp this time. What Hathaway was offering was generous payment.

"Don't heed him," the vicar pleaded. "Think of your families."

"If you are interested, come forward," Hathaway said.

The surge was so great that chairs toppled to the floor. Only the vicar and Kliskey remained where they were. Even Tremeer was offering his name.

Reverend Mr. Rosewarne rushed over to Kliskey. "Do something!"

"What?" he asked, standing. "Nobody has broken the law."

"Yet."

"You cannot arrest a man for what he is thinking."

The vicar's shoulders drooped as he nodded. His steps were heavy as he walked to the door. It closed behind him without anyone, save Kliskey, noticing.

"Well done." Neville rested his hands on the back of a chair in the vicar's cozy house.

"I would say the same to you." Reverend Mr. Rosewarne puffed on his pipe. "You have planted the seed of greed into many minds. Now we shall see what grows from that seed."

"It should not take long for the smuggler's erstwhile leader to hear about my coup d'état. I suspect he will make his displeasure known very quickly."

The vicar frowned. "You are putting Lady Priscilla and her family in danger with this scheme."

"Priscilla knows what I am doing, and she is well aware of the peril." He smiled as he pushed back from the chair. "And I have made provisions to safeguard them."

Stoddard had been aghast when Neville had outlined his need to protect those within Shadows Fall, but the butler had agreed to do everything necessary without any fanfare that might alert the leader of the smugglers. All of the servants had been told to be vigilant. Neville was depending on the fact that the smuggler's leader would not strike against the house first. The target should be Neville, and he had a few tricks of his own he could use to keep his soul within his skin.

Even so, by the time he walked into Shadows Fall's entry hall, his clothes were lathered to him with an icy sweat. Had he grown too complacent since he had assumed his title? When he had lived amid the dregs of London society, he had not hesitated to confront the most evil-minded fiends and had dared them—more than once—to halt his plans. Mayhap he was getting too old and settled in his comfortable life.

His uneasiness was, he knew as he walked up the stairs to where Priscilla waited, because of this woman. He would gladly risk his life for what he believed in, and he had many times. Yet the idea of hazarding even a single golden hair on her head sickened him.

"How did it go?" she asked.

With a moan of both desire and desperation, he pulled her to him and kissed her as he had wanted to since he saw her sitting on the boulder atop the cliff. Her slender fingers teased the hair at his nape while her other hand massaged the tight muscles across his back.

She tried to step back to ask another question, but he refused to release her. Claiming her mouth anew, he deepened the kiss until her breath pulsed swiftly against him. She was like pliable dough as his eager hands slid along her. He longed to mold her all around him.

A woman screamed.

"Aunt Cordelia!" cried Priscilla as she jerked away from Neville.

She ran toward the stairs to the upper floor. Gathering up her wrapper, she took the risers at an ungainly pace. Even so, Neville passed her before she was halfway to the top. She tried to catch up with him, but his longer legs outdistanced her quickly.

A door opened almost into her face. She jumped around it and the cat that raced past her.

Leah peered out, shouting, "What is it, Mama?"

"Stay there. You and Daphne stay in your room," she shouted over her shoulder as she saw Lady Barbara emerging into the hallway, buttoning her wrapper.

Aunt Cordelia screamed again.

Priscilla caught her aunt's heavy door as it bounced back from where Neville had slammed it open against the wall. She heard a curse and saw Neville hold her aunt as Aunt Cordelia swooned.

Aunt Cordelia swoon? What could be so appalling that it stole her aunt's senses?

Something moved on the bed. Something long and glossy and alive. It slithered across the mattress. The snake turned, its eyes glittering in the faint light.

"There is a snake here!" She did not move as it stared at her.

Neville said, "Stay with your aunt. I will see to the snake."

"Yes," she whispered. That was one order she was happy to obey. As he lowered her aunt to the floor, she added, "It may be an adder."

"More likely a smooth snake, although it should be hibernating at this time of year."

Priscilla knelt next to her aunt, rubbing Aunt Cordelia's wrists. She watched Neville step toward the bed. He was as light on his feet as a thief sneaking up on a victim. When he took a step backward and spat an oath, she stood.

"What is it?"

"Dashed cats!" He lifted a pair off the bed and set them on the floor. "How many are there in this house? Stoddard has told me he has sent more than a score to the stables."

She shooed the curious creatures away from her aunt, who would be horrified to wake and find them sniffing her. As she pushed them out the door, Neville gathered the blanket into a ball with the snake at its center.

"Be careful," she urged.

"It *is* just a smooth snake. It is harmless, Pris. I will put it out in the garden before it frightens anyone else."

"But why was it in Aunt Cordelia's bed?"

"You know why as well as I do. The timing of this prank could not be coincidental." His mouth straightened into a furious line as he walked out of the room.

Priscilla looked down at her aunt, who was regaining consciousness. When her daughters came into the room, followed closely by Lady Barbara, she put her arms around their shoulders. Calming them as Lady Barbara helped Aunt Cordelia to her feet and to a nearby chair, she hoped Neville would return quickly.

His plan to take over leadership of the smugglers must have reached their present leader even before Neville returned to Shadows Fall. The snake in Aunt Cordelia's bed could have been a warning to stop meddling. Neville would not stop until he found out who had killed Mr. Moyle and why. Priscilla knew that. What she did not know was how far the smugglers' leader would go to halt him.

NINE

Priscilla yawned as she walked into the room that now served as a breakfast parlor. Mrs. Crosby and her staff had taken on an incredible task and completed it in far less time than Priscilla deemed possible. The room had freshly aired draperies at the windows, and the furniture shone from hours of polishing. A sideboard was hidden beneath embroidered fabric that looked suspiciously like an altar cloth. Priscilla had commended Mrs. Crosby on her ingenuity more than once as additional rooms in the house were opened and aired while an inventory was taken of what might still be useable.

"Did you get any sleep last night, Mama?" Leah asked as she rose from the table to give her mother a morning kiss.

"Not much. I hope you and your sister got more."

"How is Aunt Cordelia?"

"She is doing better." That was the truth, although her aunt was furious beyond words that someone had played such a prank on her. "Lady Barbara has been much help in calming her."

"That is because, when her friend is present, Aunt Cordelia wants to show she is not weak."

Priscilla smiled. "You are a perceptive girl, but you

would be wise not to speak so in your great-aunt's hearing."

"I would never!" She put her hand over her mouth and giggled. "I would not have guessed Aunt Cordelia was frightened of snakes. I had thought they would be afraid of her."

"Leah, you should not say such things about your great-aunt," she scolded, although she had to agree. Aunt Cordelia could daunt everyone—save Neville—with a glance. "You would be scared, too, if you saw something squirming in your bed."

"Not me, Mama. I did not swoon when Isaac put that snake in my bedroom cupboard. I never thought Aunt Cordelia would surrender to vapors at the sight of a mere snake."

"Leah, that is enough." Her lips twitched, and she knew her scolding was useless. Her children loved their great-aunt dearly, but Aunt Cordelia's insistence on proper behavior at all times—an impossible goal for a child, in Priscilla's estimation—caused them to delight in the less-than-proper reaction.

Leah nodded, but giggled again as she went back to the table.

Going to the sideboard, Priscilla helped herself to two muffins waiting in a covered basket. She took them to the table and sat with her daughter. Leah had begun studying geography after the Christmas holidays, and she was enthused with the subject, chattering like a frantic squirrel.

Priscilla listened with half an ear as she wondered what the results of last night's hoax would be. Aunt Cordelia already had been unhappy at Shadows Fall and hinted several times that the betrothal ball should be moved to Thornycroft, her home in Bath. After finding a snake among her blankets, Aunt Cordelia was sure to be more insistent about leaving Cornwall.

She smiled when Lady Barbara came into the room with a swirl of her morning gown. It was an outrageous green with lace at its hem to match the ones on her sprigged mobcap. The garments would have been more suitable for Leah, but Priscilla reminded herself that she did not know what was à la mode this year. Mayhap such an extravagant color would be worn by all women during the current Season.

"Good morning. Good morning," Lady Barbara said with a broad smile. "How are you on this lovely day?"

Priscilla glanced at the windows, where low clouds and a few snowflakes suggested a storm might be on its way. The sea was the same dull shade as the sky, and tree branches were swaying in the rising wind.

Lady Barbara did not wait for an answer. As she selected food for her breakfast, she talked even more than Leah had. She sat facing Priscilla and did not seem to notice when Leah rose and excused herself.

Priscilla waited with patience while Lady Barbara outlined her suggestions for the betrothal ball, which did not, Priscilla was both pleased and puzzled to note, include returning to Aunt Cordelia's house in Bath. If her aunt had thought Lady Barbara would help her in the plans to leave Cornwall, Aunt Cordelia was sadly mistaken.

"Your aunt is sleeping well," Lady Barbara said abruptly.

"So I was told when I went to her door this morning. That is a relief. Neville is having the foundations checked for holes where a snake might have entered, but it could have been in the house before we arrived."

"It would behoove us to have our beds examined each night before retiring."

"An excellent idea."

Lady Barbara pressed her hand against her bodice. "Cordelia is a dear friend, and I was greatly distressed to see her in such a senseless state. I—Good morning, Sir Neville."

Before Priscilla could turn in her chair, broad fingers settled on her shoulders. Neville kissed her cheek and murmured, "Good morning to you, sweetheart." He stood as he added at his customary volume, "Good morning, Lady Barbara. You appear to have enjoyed a fine night's rest."

"Yes, thank you. Will you join us?" Lady Barbara gave him a warm smile.

"I regret I cannot. Pris, I am set to show you the work you were asking about last evening."

Priscilla started to ask what he was talking about, then saw his eyes shift toward Lady Barbara. Coming to her feet, she said, "That is wonderful, Neville. Lady Barbara, if you will excuse us . . ."

"Go!" she said with an imperious wave. "You have many details to tend to before the betrothal ball. Do recall what I suggested to you."

"I will," Priscilla replied, searching her mind for anything that the older woman had said worth heeding. There was not much. Putting her hand on Neville's proffered arm beneath the dark brown coat he wore over buckskin breeches, she let him lead her out into the hallway.

"You are welcome." Neville chuckled.

"Welcome?"

"For being saved from Lady Barbara's palaver. That woman could try a saint's patience with her opinions."

"She is my aunt's friend."

"So now we have two of them telling us what we should and should not do."

Priscilla smiled. "It is difficult to be angry with them when they have good intentions."

"It may be difficult for *you* . . ." He grimaced.

"Have some forbearance. Aunt Cordelia believes she is surrounded by people who have misplaced their common sense."

As they walked down the stairs, Neville glanced back in the direction of the breakfast parlor. "Mayhap Lady Barbara's good sense will change your aunt's opinion."

"Nothing changes Aunt Cordelia's mind unless she wishes it to." When they crossed the foyer and went through a doorway opening onto a corridor leading toward the east wing of the house, she asked, "Where are we bound?"

"I have found some items I believe might interest you."

Priscilla asked questions about what he had discovered, but he refused to answer, saying only that she had to see these items for herself. When he paused in front of a door, she saw the rest of the corridor was dusty and draped in spider webs. He must have explored only this far.

"*Voilà,*" he said, opening the door.

She stared at the collection filling the room. Books were stacked on chairs set in front of crates covered with filthy cloths. She flinched when she saw someone looking at her, then realized it must be a mummy case. It sat, half opened, in the back corner. It was not as grand as the one she had seen in the British Museum, because this mummy case had little of its original paint. Broken serving dishes and statues were stacked in a haphazard mélange on the seats beneath the windows lining one side of the room.

"What a jumble!" she exclaimed.

"Far more than you realize, but I have found some amazing things in here." He grinned like a child with a treat. "Look at this."

Priscilla sneezed as Neville lifted a cloth off a crate. It was not as dusty as the others, and she knew he had been searching through the room. He opened the top of the crate. Bottles were stacked inside it. Their labels were hidden by dirt, but she did not need to see them.

"Are all the crates filled with wine?" she asked.

"I have found a few with brandy." He pointed toward the mummy case. "There are several behind that, and I cannot get them out without moving the case. It weighs as much as a carriage-and-four, so I need to get some help."

"This confirms the stories about the Hathaways being involved with smuggling."

He put his hand over his heart as a grief-stricken expression lengthened his face. "My dear Priscilla, I am hurt by your lack of faith in my esteemed ancestors. You are making an assumption when it could be simply that this room was used for storage."

She laughed. "Esteemed is a word I have never heard associated with your ancestors, Neville."

"True." He wiped his hands on his breeches. "It appears the previous baronet was involved, because some of these crates have not been here for more than a few years." Lifting out a bottle, he blew on it, then sneezed as dust danced around him. "Dash it! This had better be good wine."

Squatting, she pulled in her light blue morning dress so it did not brush against the dirty crate. "If the bottles inside match the vintner's name on the crate, you should enjoy it."

He looked, whistled a single note, then put the bottle back in the crate. "I suppose if you are going to break the King's laws and risk a hempen noose, you should do so for a very good reason."

"Sir Neville?" asked Ennis from the doorway. The footman was staring in astonishment at the room.

"Yes?"

"Professor Dyson is in the parlor, sir. He requests a chance to speak to you about further excavations."

Neville nodded. "Tell him I will be there as soon as possible."

"Yes, sir." The footman raced back toward the inhabited section of the house.

"It appears, Pris, we shall have to cut our own explorations short this morning." He gave her a rakish grin. "Mayhap later we can seek out some rooms where no one can find us."

"Who knows what we might discover there?" she returned as saucily.

"Who knows indeed."

Neville scowled into his glass of wine. It was not the fine vintage he had ferreted out in the storage room. Although not as bitter as the wine he had ordered not to be served again, it was unexceptional.

Mayhap it was his mood that was bitter tonight. His plans to spend yesterday and today with Priscilla had been thwarted doubly. Both days, Professor Dyson had insisted he come out to where Dyson and his assistant were overturning the earth in hopes of finding something else interesting. By the time he returned to Shadows Fall this afternoon, Lady Cordelia had cornered Priscilla and made it very clear that Neville was not welcome to be part of their conversation about the betrothal ball. He might have argued, but Priscilla had seconded the request, and he guessed she wanted to assure herself that her aunt was recovered from her fright.

In the past two days, he had watched for another sign that the smugglers' leader was about to threaten the household. There had been nothing. Had the snake in Lady Cordelia's bed nothing to do with the smugglers? He was not ready to concede to that yet. Even if the snake had not been put there at their leader's order, the man had to do something to counter Neville's claim as the new leader of the smugglers.

What would it be?

He looked across the parlor. Lady Cordelia and Lady Barbara were conversing too low for him to hear. With the ladies, none of them speaking a word, were Priscilla and her daughters. Leah's face screwed up as she tried to halt a yawn, but it escaped anyhow. He was not surprised when Priscilla used the yawn as an excuse to interrupt the conversation.

"Sleep well, Leah," she said, kissing her daughter on the forehead.

"Yes, Mama."

Neville smiled at the girl as she went with rare speed toward the door where he stood. It was most unlike Leah to be willing to go to bed early, so she must be eager to escape the conversation. When Daphne stood, offering to make sure her sister was comfortable, he laughed quietly.

"You will rescue Mama, won't you?" Daphne whispered as she walked past him.

"I will endeavor to do so, although it takes a very

brave man to approach those town tabbies." He winked at her. "Or a very want-witted one."

Daphne giggled, then clapped her hand over her mouth so that the sound would not alert her great-aunt and Lady Barbara. As she took her sister's hand and hurried up the stairs before they were called back to explain their amusement, their lighthearted voices trickled back down the steps.

Neville smiled as he thought of the young bucks who would be bewitched by Daphne. He had first met Priscilla when she was not much older than her daughter was now, so he understood how golden hair and a musical laugh could bamboozle a man into doing things he had never considered. Things like asking her to marry him and share the rest of her life with him.

"Sir Neville?" asked Stoddard from behind him.

He turned to see his butler was not alone. Beddlemere was dressed in prime twig, looking ready to spend an evening with the *ton* in London.

"I hope I am not intruding," the marquess said, "by coming here without an invitation."

"No doubt we shall enjoy the informality," Neville said, shaking the man's hand. Having Beddlemere here would divert Lady Barbara's attention and give Priscilla a respite from her well-meaning suggestions about the betrothal ball. He hoped the marquess would recall his manners in the ladies' presence. "Come in and join the ladies."

Beddlemere needed no further urging. He went to where the women sat. He bowed over one hand, then the next, and the next. He somehow managed to sit next to Lady Cordelia on the settee with Lady Barbara in a chair on his right.

Priscilla rose and walked to where Neville still stood. With a smile, she asked, "Are you going to join us?"

"I was hoping to devise some excuse not to."

"Do not be down-pinned, Neville."

He curved his hand along her cheek. "I shall not be once this betrothal ball is past, and I do not have to share you with your so-called helpers."

"Then there will be the wedding to plan."

"Mayhap a drive to Gretna Green is in order."

She rolled her eyes. "Do not even suggest that as a jest. Aunt Cordelia would be outraged, and I would never hear the end of it."

"Such an irresponsible woman," he said, mimicking her aunt's tone, "cannot be expected to raise an earl."

Priscilla laughed, and he drank in the sound. It was so filled with joy that his dreary spirits were banished. He went with her to where Beddlemere was filling his glass. Refilling it, he noted. The glass the marquess held had drops of wine in the bottom.

As he sat Priscilla next to him on the settee facing his neighbor and her aunt, Neville said, "Forgive the vintage, Beddlemere. Not the best."

"Do you mean the rest of the wine stored in this house is gone?" the marquess asked.

"I have not checked the cellar myself." He felt Priscilla stiffen next to him as she watched Beddlemere with a smile. "I have been busy."

"So I hear."

"Hear?"

"Quite the performance you and the vicar put on at the tavern in Trepoole a few nights ago."

"Performance?" asked Lady Cordelia. "I thought you had put aside your work in the theater when you assumed your title. It is not appropriate."

Neville was astonished when Beddlemere took Lady Cordelia's hand and patted it gently. The marquess said,

"Do not let my comments disturb you, Lady Cordelia. I spoke out of hand, and I apologize. A discussion of what took place at that low tavern is not befitting your ears."

"But if he said or did anything to bring shame to the family—"

"No one could tarnish your mirror-perfect reputation," he gushed.

Lady Cordelia smiled, amazing Neville, who had not guessed she was susceptible to blatant flattery. "You are very kind, Lord Beddlemere."

"Robert, if you will indulge me in such familiarity."

"Of course. You must address me as Cordelia." She flushed and hastily added, "And my niece as Priscilla."

"I am greatly honored."

"Now tell me about what *he* did at the tavern."

Neville listened as Beddlemere gave a very white-washed version of what had been said at the tavern in Trepoole. Some of the facts were altered and others wrong, but he did not correct the marquess. Beside him, Priscilla remained silent, too. When he glanced at her, she was staring at Lady Barbara.

He looked at the woman, who was being ignored. Not happily, if he were to judge by the set of her lips. Each time Beddlemere gave Lady Cordelia a compliment, Lady Barbara's mouth grew more taut.

"Foxed? *He* was foxed among the villagers?" Lady Cordelia's sharp voice brought his attention back to her. She was scowling at him. "Priscilla, I hope you are listening."

"To every word," Priscilla replied. Giving Beddlemere a scintillating smile, she went on. "This afternoon, Professor Dyson was showing Neville some of the shards he has uncovered. Fascinating when one thinks of how long they have been buried beneath the earth."

"Priscilla—" her aunt began.

"Aunt Cordelia, the professor was saying he hoped to find some amulets among the pottery shards. Can you imagine? The jewelry a Roman matron would have worn a millennium and a half ago. What a sight that would be if Daphne could wear a piece when she is fired off!"

Beddlemere's brows rose. "You believe Dyson will find something of other than academic value in the fields?"

"He has found some coins already," Neville answered, glad to help Priscilla change the subject. "I believe several gold ones."

"I had heard only of some small pieces of silver."

"You would have to ask the professor, but I am certain he spoke of gold coins. He believes the lost settlement was once a market town." He refilled the marquess's glass as well as Lady Barbara's. The lady snatched hers from the table and glowered while she drank. "It seems logical to believe he will find some items of value."

Beddlemere murmured, "I had not considered that."

"An ancient pendant would look lovely on Daphne," Priscilla said with a smile. "There are some interesting pieces at the British Museum, and if Daphne wore something like those, she would catch the notice of everyone in attendance at her first assembly."

Lady Cordelia leaned forward. "You have asked the professor to alert us the moment he finds something like that, haven't you?"

When Priscilla jabbed him with a concealed elbow, Neville realized belatedly that the lady was speaking to him.

"I doubt," he said, "anyone could keep Professor Dyson from alerting everyone in the shire."

"Imagine. My great-niece wearing something so unusual at her first gathering."

"Such finery is not necessary." Beddlemere patted her hand again. "She is sure to catch every man's eye, for she has inherited much of your beauty, Cordelia."

"You are too kind."

"If truth is kind, then I am kind." He squeezed her hand as he drained his glass again. "I regret having to bring my call to an end, but it was beginning to snow again as I arrived at the door. My coachman complains about driving in the snow." He stood. "Not that I can comprehend why. Snow is easier to drive through than the quagmire when the roads soften with spring."

"Do call again," Lady Cordelia said with a smile. "It is a pleasure to have a gentleman join us for our evening's conversation."

Neville heard Priscilla's soft laugh. He swallowed his own at how deftly the lady had insulted him at the same time she complimented Beddlemere.

The marquess bid them a good evening. He seemed unaware that Lady Barbara had not spoken a word since he sat down next to Lady Cordelia. Either he was too much in his cups to notice, or he simply did not care.

"Hathaway?" The marquess motioned with his head toward the door.

Neville set himself on his feet. "Excuse me, ladies."

He followed Beddlemere into the hallway and down the stairs. When a footman came forward with the marquess's hat and cloak and said something quietly as he bowed his head, Beddlemere glanced at him and then at Neville.

"Thank you, Ennis," Neville said. "There will be nothing else now."

The lad bowed and went through one of the shadowed doors.

"A word of warning," Beddlemere said as he hooked his cape over his shoulders. "You may have thought you were having a good joke on the bumpkins in Trepoole, but smuggling is no joke here."

"Is that so?"

"Those men will expect you to bring them booty, Hathaway. If you fail, they will be furious. At the same time, you are disrupting the balance along the shore with claims to what you believe are your family's rights."

"Believe? There is a long tradition between the Hathaways and shipping along the north shore of Cornwall."

Beddlemere put his nose close to Neville's. His winesoured breath billowed out on his words. "You are playing with fire, Hathaway. Take heed of my warning before it is too late."

"Too late?" If he kept Beddlemere talking, he might learn something to help explain if the smugglers had had a hand in Moyle's death.

"You have heard the tales as I have. Men disappearing without a trace. Lives ruined." The marquess looked up the stairs. "You have a lovely fiancée and two charming future stepdaughters. I would hate to hear something horrible had happened to them."

Neville said nothing as Beddlemere opened the door and went out, leaving the door ajar. Snowflakes blew in on the wind.

The wind was icy, but not as cold as the fear within Neville. He must be doubly cautious from this point onward in protecting Priscilla and her family. Bed-dlemere might enjoy flirting with the ladies, but he was no fool. He was scared to his bones and believed Neville should be, too, now that he had challenged the smugglers' leader.

TEN

"You are being silly."

Priscilla knew better than to speak when her aunt assumed that tone. For once, Aunt Cordelia was saying those words to someone else, but Priscilla could take no satisfaction in it.

Lady Barbara was weeping, her handkerchief held close to her face as she dabbed at her eyes and blew her nose. "How could you, Cordelia? You know my long acquaintance with Robert Beddlemere."

"I did nothing to encourage him."

"You acted like a coquette." She flung her hand toward Priscilla. "You acted no better than if you were as young and untutored as one of her daughters."

Wanting to defend her daughters, Priscilla reminded herself of the wisdom of saying nothing. This was between her aunt and Lady Barbara. Getting involved in the brangle would likely end up with both women peeved at her.

"You should not speak so of Daphne and Leah," Aunt Cordelia fired back.

"I was not speaking of them. I was speaking of *you*." Lady Barbara lowered her handkerchief from her face. "I shall not speak *to* you again." She went toward the door.

Aunt Cordelia looked at Priscilla, then followed her

friend. Priscilla understood what her aunt had not needed to say. Last night, Lady Barbara had stayed with Aunt Cordelia, making sure she had recovered her wits before Lady Barbara sought her own bed. That was a debt that could not go unpaid, and her aunt hated owing anyone else a duty.

Priscilla stood and rubbed her lower back. She had spent too many hours sitting while Aunt Cordelia berated her. Mayhap Neville was right when he said she gave her aunt too much latitude. The ache in her back bounced to her forehead, and Priscilla massaged it. Bother! She did not need a headache tonight. A good night's sleep would put everything into perspective, even Aunt Cordelia's determination to have the world made exactly to her specifications.

Going to the windows overlooking the sea, she saw through the falling snowflakes the light from a ship. It was headed west toward Land's End and the vast ocean beyond and was too far offshore to be involved with smugglers.

"At least not here," she said aloud.

"What is not here?" asked Neville from across the room.

She faced him and smiled. The pain in her head eased as he walked toward her carrying two glasses. He held one out to her.

"More wine?" she asked. "Another glass, and I shall be as drunk as a lord." She chuckled. "Or a baronet at the village tavern."

"I portrayed a man far drunker than a lord. As drunk as an emperor would be a better description."

"No wonder Lord Beddlemere felt it necessary to come here to offer you a warning not to act so foolishly again. He seems familiar with the ways of the smugglers."

"Were you eavesdropping on us, Pris?"

She smiled. "As soon as he brought up the topic of your visit to the tavern, it was obvious why Lord Beddlemere was calling."

"His family has had an estate along the shore almost as long as the Hathaway family has. If my ancestors were smuggling, you can be sure his were as well."

"And he is following that family tradition as you are pretending you are yours?"

"It would be astonishing if he was not. Smuggling can be very profitable."

"You sound as if you are actually considering participating in it."

He laughed. "It is tempting, but I fear I am too much a law-abiding citizen of the realm now to take part in such crimes."

Smiling again, she took a sip of the wine. She looked down into the glass, astonished. "This is better than what was served earlier."

"I instructed Stoddard to get some bottles from the storage room. I find I prefer it." He tapped his glass against hers, sending a crystal chime swirling through the room. "And I prefer this company as well, Pris."

She sat on a bench beside the window and paid no mind to the cold coming around the glass. "You need not continue with Lord Beddlemere's Spanish coin. The man is getting himself in deep trouble."

"With Lady Barbara?"

"Yes. She did not appreciate his attentions to my aunt."

He laughed. "Pris, you have spent too many years away from the Polite World if you fail to recognize one of man's oldest tricks. Beddlemere hopes to make Lady Barbara jealous so she will return to his bed."

"Return?" she choked.

"I have taken your advice and listened to what the servants are saying. Apparently Lady Barbara was out very, very late on her first night here."

"Very late?"

"Arriving back just before dawn. The past two nights she has remained within the walls of Shadows Fall. A most intriguing fact, when *on dits* hint she has been his mistress for several years."

She tapped her chin. "Which suggests she may have tired of waiting for him to propose, so she has threatened to leave him. That makes no sense. They were laughing together on the shore when we met them while speaking with the professor and Mr. Randall."

"But he has not called since. Who knows what she might have said to him later?"

"True, and now he is trying to make her jealous by pretending to be interested in another woman."

"That could be Beddlemere's ploy."

Priscilla shook her head. "I wish I could agree, but his interest in my aunt seemed quite genuine."

"His interest in the fortune left to her by three wealthy husbands mayhap." He took a deep drink and smiled.

"Must you always be so cynical?"

"It is in my nature to question everything, and I have to question Beddlemere's sudden interest in your aunt."

She laughed. "Be honest, Neville, and own that you cannot imagine anyone finding my aunt appealing because you are accustomed to her dressing you down."

"There is that aspect." He smiled. "You ruined my own ploy, Pris."

"And what ploy was that?"

"To persuade you that you need someone to look

after you because you cannot even recognize when a man is trying to seduce your aunt."

"That makes no sense."

His smile faded. "Nothing does now, Pris."

"What exactly did Lord Beddlemere have to say to you after you left?"

"Nothing new."

"About the smugglers?"

"Dash it, Pris! Must you always be so astute?"

"I must be when you speak in circles. I wish to speak plainly."

"As I do." He put his boot on the bench beside her. Resting his elbow on his knee, he smiled at her. "To own the truth, I would rather not speak at all."

She gazed up into his dark eyes, which were as mysterious as the night. Within them were regions she did not yet dare to explore, but the very thought sent a thrill cascading through her. She laced her fingers through his as he set his glass on the wide sill. Taking hers, he put it beside his before drawing her to her feet.

His arm encircled her waist and drew her against him. His other hand cupped her chin. He tilted it back so she could not evade the powerful emotions in his eyes. She did not want to evade them. She wanted to revel in them, sharing each one. As his thumb moved along her jaw, he smiled.

"Pris." His rough voice when he spoke her name was as gentle as his fingertip against her cheek. He whispered her name again before his mouth caressed hers.

With a moan, she gave herself to the kiss. His tongue slipped along her lips, and she delved her own deep within his mouth. Her fingers tightened on his coat as every inch of her begged her to forget they had yet to speak their marriage vows.

He must have been thinking much the same because he raised his head and whispered, "Haven't I told you there is only so much a man can endure?"

"Or a woman."

His smile sent more delight through her. "I like hearing that, Pris."

Stepping away, she gave him a smile. "I wager you do."

Neville did not answer. He was peering out the window at the lights from the ship.

"It is passing by," Priscilla said.

"I am not so sure of that." He started for the door.

She ran after him. "Give me time to get my cloak and—"

"Sweetheart, you cannot go with me."

"You cannot go alone."

"I will take Riley with me."

She laughed at the image of his valet wandering about the shore in the midst of a snowstorm. "He will be useless."

Pausing, he nodded. "I have to agree. I will take Stoddard."

"He will not go. He has not left the house since we arrived. Can you imagine his perfectly shined shoes on that slippery path to the shore?"

"Dash it! He works for me, not the other way around."

"I will go with—"

He grasped her shoulders. "You cannot go. I need to have you here to keep watch on your daughters and aunt."

"That is an excuse to prevent me from going with you. With a houseful of servants, no one could sneak in here."

"Not even to put a snake in your aunt's bed or to pretend to be some sort of ghost?"

Priscilla faltered. He was right, although she loathed

owning to that. "Take someone with you who knows the cliffs."

"I will."

"And let me know what you find."

"At breakfast—"

"Tonight! Do you think I could sleep without knowing that you have returned safely?"

"And what I have found?" When he folded her hands between his, he pressed them to his chest, bringing her even closer. She wondered if his skin was on fire, for it kindled something hot and sweet on hers.

She smiled. "You know me too well, Neville."

His fingers drifted across her shoulder before trailing down her back. "Not yet, sweetheart, but I am looking forward to the night when I can say I know you very, very well."

Priscilla folded her arms in front of her to keep her hands from reaching out to him. He gave her a swift, fiery kiss before he rushed down the stairs. Hearing him call for Ennis, she blew out the lamp and went up the stairs to her room. It might be a long wait.

"Is there anything else, my lady?"

Priscilla smiled and waved tiredly toward the door. It had been almost four hours since Neville had left. Four hours of pacing and looking out the window and listening for his return. Four hours of being disappointed.

"Nothing else, Glenda," she said to her abigail. "Go to bed. I know you must be exhausted."

The rotund woman nodded. "Good night, my lady."

When the door closed, Priscilla went to the window beyond her bed and looked out as she had a score of times tonight. No lights marked the strand, and the ship had been swallowed by the storm. If it had come closer, she had seen no sign. Mayhap Neville's arrival on the shore had changed the captain's plan to meet the smugglers.

But why wasn't he back yet?

He might be negotiating with the captain who had come ashore in a small boat. He might be continuing with his plan to become the new leader of the smugglers. He might have had to go into Trepoole for either reason or another one entirely. He might have . . .

She sighed. She could come up with dozens of reasons why he was still gone, but until she knew the truth it was senseless to consider these scenarios. Neville would come to her room as soon as he returned. They would talk about whatever had kept him away so long, and that discussion would take up even more of the night. Getting some sleep now was what she should do.

Even knowing that, Priscilla found it impossible to relax. Her pillows seemed too soft; then they were too hard. The blanket was too hot, but when she kicked it aside, her feet became chilled. She stared out the window at the snowflakes, hoping their hypnotic dance would lull her to sleep. Instead she saw ice pellets strike the window. She thought of how cold it must be outside and wondered how slippery the cliff path was. Turning to stare at the door with its thin line of light edging around it on three sides reminded her how she wanted to see it open as Neville came in. Eventually even that light was extinguished.

I should have gone with him. That thought repeated endlessly in her mind.

Priscilla heard a noise. Not a noise but the groan she had heard the first night she slept at Shadows Fall. She sat up in bed. It came from outside the house. There had been no time to investigate the sound, because Mr. Moyle's death and the smugglers had occupied them. Mayhap they should have taken time to find out what was causing it.

Another sound came, soft and furtive and much closer. Was that Neville returning, sneaking to her room so her aunt would not discover him here? The noise came again. It was *within* her room. Trying to block out the tap of sleet against the panes, she listened so intently her ears ached. She strained to see, but the room was a collection of shadows, darker and lighter, concealing everything. She could not see anything. Because there was nothing to see, she reminded herself as she pulled her blanket to her chin and wished she was in her cozy room in Stonehall-on-Sea.

Hinges shrieked in the silence, but she did not see the hallway door move. Was someone opening her cupboard? She could not recall it making such a harsh sound.

"Neville?"

There was no answer. She held her breath, waiting for the sound to come again.

"Don't be silly!" she chided herself in a whisper. By this time, she should be acclimated to the various voices of the house settling at night. How Neville would laugh at her skittishness! More stealthy footsteps. Not from outside in the corridor, but from within the room. She reached for her wrapper as she scanned the room. Only the outline of the window was visible. Someone else was in the room.

"Neville?" she called.

No answer.

"Glenda?" Mayhap her abigail had heard the groan and had come to check on her.

A silhouette appeared before the gray window. She remained silent. She wanted to find out who was skulking through her room in the middle of the night. If she screamed, Neville's valet might hear, but she wanted the intruder to think she was now so frightened she could not utter a whisper.

The figure moved away from the window, but she followed him as he edged through the dark room. He was coming toward her bed. If this was Neville's idea of a hoax . . . No, he would not tease her when he knew she was already unsettled.

The person walked toward the bed with unswerving steps. Then light flashed in her eyes. She held up her hands and cried out in astonishment. A hand emerged from the light. She stared, immobilized with fear, as she saw the ring on his left forefinger. It had been on the hand of the dead man when she saw him in the mound.

"You cannot be Gab Moyle," she choked. Even if there were phantoms prowling the passages of Shadows Fall, they would belong to the house. Gab Moyle's spirit would not leave his resting place in the village to come here.

She reached for her lamp. When she threw it at the hand, the fingers vanished back into the light. Abrupt darkness blinded her again. The window crashed open. Sleet swirled through the room.

Priscilla jumped out of bed and ran to the window. She slipped on water on the floor and grasped the footboard, so she did not fall. No ghost left wet footprints. She knelt and dipped her fingers in the water. Holding it to her nose, she frowned. It smelled of salt. Whoever had left water behind must have been on the strand. One of the smugglers? She shuddered as she thought of them wandering freely about Shadows Fall.

She must find out the truth. Flinging her wrapper over her shoulders, she thrust her hands through the clinging sleeves as she rushed to the door. She yanked it open and cried out in horror when she saw a body huddled in front of it. Blood stained the floor beneath dark hair.

"Neville!" she cried.

Dropping to her knees, she ran her hands along his arms and legs. Nothing was broken. Carefully, she lifted his head. Her hands became as scarlet as the hair near his right temple. He had been struck on the head. Placing his head gently on the floor, she ran along the hallway to his room.

Riley appeared within seconds of her pounding on the door. Her expression must have told him something terrible had happened because before she could speak, he was racing toward where Neville was sprawled on the floor.

"I will get help to get him to his bed," Riley said.

"Go! Quickly!"

Priscilla sat cross-legged and cradled Neville's head in her lap. He did not so much as groan. If she had not seen the excruciatingly slow rise and fall of his chest, she would have feared he was dead.

"Stay alive," she whispered. "I cannot lose you, too."

He did not answer then and remained silent when Riley returned with several footmen and Stoddard. The butler directed the footmen to lift Neville and carry him to his room. Riley assisted Priscilla to her feet and into Neville's chamber, for which she was grateful. As much as her knees wobbled, she doubted she could have gotten there on her own.

The room was much smaller than hers, and the large tester bed took up most of the floor. Its surface was so high, she feared the men would not be able to lift Neville onto the bed. Somehow they managed.

She pulled up a stool to stand on as lamps were lit. She heard the sharp gasps when the men saw the red marks on his face, marks left by knuckles.

"Someone beat him hard," Riley said, his voice shaking even more than her knees.

"More than one person, I would assume. Neville can hold his own against any single foe." She directed the footmen to bring water and cloths so she could bandage the wound on his head. A quick examination told her it must have been caused by a grazing blow. If he had been struck as hard there as on his face, he would be dead.

Just like Gab Moyle.

She refused to think of that while she wrapped his head, holding it up while Riley put a clean pillow beneath him. She did not look at the bloody one.

"What can I bring for you, my lady?" Stoddard asked, wringing his hands.

She wished her own butler were here instead of in London, waiting for them to return to Bedford Square. Gilbert would have known what to do without asking. So many times he had tended to bruises on Isaac, who had tried to climb all the trees in Stonehall-on-Sea and seemed intent on scraping every inch of himself.

"Bring some wine from the storage room," she ordered.

"Which storage room?"

"Ennis will know." She looked around the room. "Where is Ennis?"

"I sent him for more clean cloths. He was of little use limping around the room."

"Limping? Was he hurt, too, by those who struck Sir Neville?"

"I did not ask. I am sorry if that was a mistake."

She put her hand on the butler's trembling arm. "Ask him to bring some bottles from the crates in the storage room. Then send someone to the stillroom to fetch some viper's bugloss. It needs to be put in boiling water for about a half hour to make a tisane to ease the headache Sir Neville is sure to have when he awakens. Also have a hops tea prepared in case he cannot sleep from the pain."

"May we bring something for you, my lady?"

"Bring two glasses for the wine, for I shall need some before the night is past, I am certain." She smiled weakly.

Stoddard stopped kneading his hands together and smiled back. "We shall have everything you ordered brought as quickly as possible."

"But quietly. Do not wake my daughters or my aunt or Lady Barbara."

"Lady Barbara is not within the house tonight," the butler said, flushing.

Priscilla gave him a sympathetic smile, then glanced toward the bed. She could not fret about Lady Barbara and her lover now. "Then ask the staff not to disturb my aunt and daughters. There is no need for a hullabaloo."

The butler nodded and shooed the footmen out ahead of him. Only the rustle of whispers came from the corridor.

Riley cleared his throat. "Can I get you something else from your cupboard, my lady?"

Priscilla looked down at her bloodstained wrapper. She suspected her nightgown was crimson, too. "Please wake Glenda and have her bring me whatever she planned to have ready in the morning."

"Right away, my lady."

When he slipped out, she went to the bed. She wondered if she had ever seen Neville's face appear so gray and lifeless beneath an ebony shadow of whiskers. It was always vibrant with life, his expressions by turn mirroring or hiding his thoughts. She brushed aside the stubborn strand of hair that dropped into his eyes.

"Ouch," he mumbled.

She jerked back her fingers. "Neville? Neville, are you awake?"

"I hope to perdition not. I hope this pain is part of a nightmare."

In spite of herself, she smiled. Trust Neville to hold on to his bizarre sense of humor even when he was hurt.

"I am afraid this is no nightmare," she said. "You are awake."

"Dash it!" He opened his eyes and winced. "How did I get back to Shadows Fall?"

"I was hoping you could tell me. I found you unconscious outside my door when I was trying to figure out who was creeping through my room, pretending to be Gab Moyle's restless spirit."

"Creeping? Spirit?" He started to push himself up to sit, then groaned.

She put her hand on his shoulder. "You should not exert yourself. You have been hurt."

Shaking off her hand, he sat. He cradled his head in his hands even as he demanded, "Are you telling me someone was in your room tonight?"

"Yes, but, Neville, it is not as important as making sure you do not hurt yourself more."

"Let me decide what is important." He raised his head.

"Do not get disagreeably high in the instep with me, Neville Hathaway! You have been pummeled, and as it appears to have knocked all sense out of your head, then you need to heed me."

She was shocked when he grinned and said, "Yes, Lady Priscilla." It was a faint grin, but a grin nonetheless.

"Mayhap I should have hoped someone would knock some sense *into* your thick skull."

"A pointless wish."

"What happened to you?"

Neville's explanation was quick, even though he paused frequently to close his eyes as pain slashed across his face. He had gone with Ennis down to the shore to see if the ship was sailing past or the lights were a signal to the smugglers. The path had been icy, and Ennis had fallen down, slicing open his knee.

"So that is why he was limping," she said.

"There was blood running down his leg, Pris, so I sent him back to the house."

"And continued on your own? Did you ever consider that it was stupid to go on your own?"

"Yes, I did consider it, but I went anyhow." He leaned his head back against the bed and stared up at the ceiling. "I believed the storm would conceal me."

"But it concealed your attackers instead."

"Pris, you are developing an irritating habit of jumping ahead to the end of the story."

"Did you see any of their faces?"

He shook his head, then groaned. "I did not even see their fists until they struck me. The man I saw wore a mask with slits for the eyes. There were at least three of them because two held my arms behind my back while the other tried to beat me senseless. I pretended he had, and the two behind me let me fall." He touched the bandage around his head. "I must have hit my head on a rock. That is the last thing I remember until I opened my eyes to see your pretty face."

"At the same time, the phantom came to my room with what looked like the ring the Moyles wear."

"So you were to think Gab Moyle had come to haunt you?" He laughed weakly. "You are too lucid to believe that."

"I was not too lucid for a moment. It was bone-chilling to see it on a hand reaching out toward me." She looked at the door as it opened.

Stoddard entered, followed by Ennis, who was limping slightly. The footman wore a rueful expression as he set a tray with two teapots on the windowsill.

"Riley asked me to tell you, my lady, that he is still waiting for your abigail to gather what you requested," the butler said. "You appear much better, sir."

"Being left for dead outside Lady Priscilla's door does not enable me to look my best."

"Neville," she chided. This was not the time to beleaguer his far too serious butler.

"Thank you, Stoddard," Neville said like a chastised schoolboy.

Thanking the butler as well, she asked, "Ennis, how is your knee? Have you had someone check it for you?"

He stared at the floor. "I have, my lady."

Stoddard motioned for the footman to leave, then followed while Priscilla went around the bed. She lifted the lid on the first teapot and sniffed. That was the hops tea. Pouring from the other teapot, she held out the cup to Neville.

"What brew is this?" he asked.

"A *tisane* to relieve your headache."

He sipped and grimaced. "It may cure it by killing me."

"Do not mewl like a baby." She hurried to add when his eyes widened, "Forgive me, Neville. I did not mean to sound sharp."

"You have every reason to, Pris." He held out his arm. "Come here."

Knowing how appalled her aunt would be, but not caring, Priscilla sat on the bed next to him and let his arm encircle her shoulders. She pressed her face against his chest.

"I am sorry, Pris," he whispered against her hair.

"I was afraid I had lost you, too."

"My head is too hard for that."

"Please do not jest with me either. Not now. Not about this."

"I shall not."

She raised her head. "Promise me that you will not chase after the smugglers again like you did tonight."

"Pris, I cannot promise that."

"But why not?"

His jaw grew rigid. "Because he wants to scare us away. Your ghostly visitor, the snake in your aunt's bed, mayhap even the tower collapsing may be part of a plot to frighten us into leaving Shadows Fall so he can continue holding sway over the villagers."

"He? The leader of the smugglers?"

"Yes, and I intend to find out who he is." He touched the bandage on his head. "And repay him."

"No, you must not."

His eyes narrowed. "Pris—"

"You must not!" She sat straighter. "Neville, I know it is your habit to run headlong into danger, but it is a habit you must change. You have others to consider in addition to yourself."

He drew his arm from around her. "You and your children?"

"*Us* and the children."

"I am thinking of us. If that madman keeps up his tomfoolery, someone else could die."

"I agree. You must stop baiting him. Let the constable handle it."

"Kliskey could not find the smugglers' leader if the man wore a sign around his neck."

"Mayhap, but, Neville, you must stop." She held his hand between hers. "You must."

"I cannot."

"But I am asking you. For the sake of the children and for ours."

"I cannot, Pris. I cannot change that much."

She blinked back hot tears. "Cannot? Or is it that you simply do not wish to?"

"What does it matter?"

"It matters a great deal." She slid off the bed. "I love you, Neville, but I will not let your attempt at heroics endanger my children."

"Will not let?" His voice rose with an anger that had rarely been aimed at her. "Pris, you knew who I am when you agreed to be my wife."

"I don't know very much about you at all."

"You are being absurd enough to make a cat laugh."

"Am I?" She heard the door open, but did not turn as Riley came into the room. "What do I know of you, Neville? Most of what I know is rumor and innuendo. What is true, and what is not?"

"I thought my past did not matter to you."

"I thought so, too, but it does." Her voice broke. "It does far more than I guessed when you want to continue with your reckless life. Mayhap I have been so befuddled by love that I failed to see the truth until now."

"I have not tried to trick you in any way, Pris. I do love you."

"That you love me I am not questioning."

He reached for her hand. "You are questioning if I love you enough to change my ways?"

"Yes."

"I honestly don't know. I never have considered that question."

The tears seeped out of her eyes, and she did not wipe them away. "I know, Neville. You are happy with your life the way it is. I thought I could be happy sharing that life, but now I am not so certain. Mayhap Aunt Cordelia—"

"Was right that you marrying me would be a most mistaken thing?"

His whetted voice sliced into her, and she backed away from the bed. When she bumped into Riley, she snatched her clothing from his arms. She ran out of the room. If Neville called after her, she did not hear him, for his question echoed in her head. She had no answer.

ELEVEN

Neville sat next to the largest boulder at the water's edge. The soft foam from the waves brushed the tips of his boots, and he knew the tide was rising. He leaned one arm on the boulder and stared at the empty cove. It had not been empty last night. He could see lines among the stones where heavy crates had been unloaded and taken to wherever the smugglers hid their goods.

What an idiot he had been! He should have heeded Priscilla's warnings, but he had been determined to learn what he could about the smugglers. His lesson had been painful. The smugglers' leader had either promised even better terms to the men from Trepoole than Neville had or, more likely, had threatened them with death if they did not work for him.

He had followed the tracks until they disappeared in the middle of the cove. The smugglers had ensured that nobody would discover where they stashed their illicit wares.

Pushing himself to his feet, he groaned as pain blared in his head. Riley had been furious with him this morning, telling Neville he should remain in bed and rest. The valet had not hidden his anger either at how Neville had let Priscilla walk out last night in tears.

It could have been the wrong thing to do, but Neville knew that chasing after her would have been worse. Seeing Priscilla weep and knowing he was the cause of those tears had unnerved him. She was right. He did not want to end his efforts to find Moyle's killer and free the villagers in Trepoole from the terror that consumed their lives. He did not want to change his life, which insisted he pursue wrongdoers so they could pay for their crimes.

But he knew that was not the crux of the chasm opening between them. Priscilla shared his hatred of the strong preying on the weak, and she was as resolved as he was to banish the cloud of fear over the shore. Her tears had been brought on by her anguish about losing him and making her children suffer again as they had when Lazarus died.

How could he ask her to do that? He loved her, and, in loving her, he should want to do everything possible to keep her from pain. Mayhap that was why he had been reticent about his past. Not that he was ashamed of it, for he had done the best he could with the life he had, but he could not see what good would come of telling her of childhood hunger and desperation as well as youthful crimes. In the theater, where he had been able to put his skills of subterfuge and mimicry to good use, he had found the family denied him. Then his past caught up with him, and he was given a single chance to redeem himself. Lazarus Flanders had helped him then, and Neville knew he owed Priscilla's late husband his life and more.

He put his hand under his coat, checking that the small case remained there. It did, but he wondered now if he would be able to give Priscilla the gift he had for her. Hours of searching throughout the house had ended in success when he found this small case. A single success, because everything else was a bumblebath.

He climbed the steep path, glancing toward Shadows Fall. If he were a gentleman, he would go to Priscilla and tell her that Lady Cordelia had been right when she said their betrothal was a mistake. That way, there might be a way to salvage the friendship they had once shared. He laughed sharply. Friendship was not what he wanted with Priscilla. The very idea of giving her nothing but a chaste salute on the cheek or bowing over her fingers each time they met was ludicrous. He wanted her in his arms and sharing his bed.

Turning in the opposite direction at the top of the cliff, he walked down the hill toward where Professor Dyson might be poking about. He envied the professor his simple existence, where he could live comfortably in the past.

Neville paused by the low stone wall. If the men were working, they must be inside the mound, for he saw nobody on the overturned earth. What had this village looked like when the temple was not hidden? He would rather think of that than of what he must say to Priscilla when he returned to Shadows Fall.

It was easy to imagine petitioners climbing up the steep cliffs to bring their prayers to the gods and seek favors. No one would have dared to do anything in the village without their plans being approved by the priests.

He smiled as he tried to envision Priscilla coming to seek the god's blessing. His smile faded into a sigh at the image of her dressed in an ethereal robe. Her beauty would capture the attention of the priest. As she bowed, her golden hair would glow in the sunlight.

The priest put hands on her shoulders. Her supple

skin sent a ripple of pleasure through him as his fingers coursed up through her hair. Heat gathered deep within him when he drew her to her feet and slipped her into his arms. The thin silk of her robe would grow warm as he held her to his bare chest. With her smile promising everything he could hope for, he would take her to a private room in the depths of the temple to share the gods' gift of passion.

Neville swore as he opened his eyes. When had the fantasy priest become him? He tried to slow his breathing, but could not curb the tingling along his skin. He fisted his hands on the low wall and cursed again. He needed to think of a way to settle the differences between them.

"Sir Neville?"

He looked up to see Randall walking along the wall. Randall was wearing a heavy coat and carried some sort of pack over his right shoulder. "Good morning."

"Good morning, sir. If you do not mind me asking, what happened to you?"

"A disagreement." He touched the bruise on his left cheekbone and grimaced. "I was on the losing end, as you can see."

"I see," Randall answered, but his puzzled expression suggested just the opposite. He shifted the pack on his shoulder. "I am glad I had a chance to see you and bid you a personal good-bye. You have been very supportive of the excavations on your property."

"You are leaving?" Now it was his turn not to understand.

Randall nodded. "I am done working here."

"Why?"

"I am quitting."

"Why?" Neville asked again.

"Professor Dyson." His hands clenched. "I had thought I would learn much working with him, but all I have learned is that he knows very little about Roman settlements in Britain."

"And he is accepting of artifacts that seem to be emerging from the sea unscathed?"

"Not only that they are unscathed, but that they would belong to a settlement like the one here." He gestured toward the open field. "Other than the temple mound, we have found nothing out of the ordinary at this site. Pieces of broken pottery, a few broken weapons, and what may have been a woman's pendant. Yet he believes—and wishes to persuade you and Lord Beddlemere—that the flagons and the artifacts are a fundamental part of the site. I will not be a party to his lies."

Neville said quietly, "The professor will miss you and your hard work."

"I doubt it, for I stand in the way of proving his so-called theories." He looked over his shoulder and in every direction before adding, "I believe someone is smuggling relics from the site."

"Smuggling? We have no need for *more* smugglers, Randall."

"Stealing, then, if you will. Moyle may not have been the only thief. Farewell, Sir Neville. I am going to call on Lord Beddlemere to warn him of how Professor Dyson is duping him. I am glad I had a chance to let you know, too."

"Thank you, Randall." He watched the man's face closely as he added, "I trust you have informed Constable Kliskey of your plans to leave."

"The constable?"

"He may have some questions for you about Moyle's murder, and he should know where to reach you."

"Why should he have questions for me later when he has not asked me a single one thus far?"

Neville told himself he should not be astonished that the constable was making no effort to do his job. From what he had witnessed at the tavern, Kliskey was too frightened of the smugglers to chance infuriating them, even with the investigation of a murder.

All he said to Randall was, "Good luck to you."

"And to you." He glanced again at the mound and walked away, shaking his head.

"I am going to need it," Neville murmured as he sat on the wall and looked back at Shadows Fall. He had to do something to break this stalemate in the investigation and he had to find a way to mend his differences with Priscilla, but for the first time in his life, he was not sure what.

"Another letter accepting the invitation to the ball." Aunt Cordelia put it down on the growing pile on the table in the parlor. "I am amazed so many people are willing to travel this distance when the first events of the Season have already begun."

Priscilla picked up the letter and tried to read it. The words blurred as if tears were falling anew down her face. When Aunt Cordelia had insisted on Priscilla sitting with her this morning, it had seemed not worth the effort to resist. She needed all her strength to pretend that nothing was amiss when everything around her was falling apart. If she had realized Aunt Cordelia was going to go through the letters delivered to Shadows

Fall, she might have found some excuse not to join her. It was too late now.

She shivered at the thought. She hoped it was not too late to salvage something from the disaster the betrothal had become.

Lady Barbara took the letter from Priscilla and scanned it. Priscilla had been amazed to see Lady Barbara waiting in the parlor. Aunt Cordelia must have patched up her friendship with her bosom bow. Wanting to ask how when Lady Barbara must have returned to the house only a few hours before, Priscilla said nothing that would reveal she knew of Lady Barbara's late night excursions.

"Everyone is curious to discover if Sir Neville will actually go through with the betrothal," Lady Barbara said with a laugh.

"Or back out?" Aunt Cordelia's eyes glittered with hope.

Priscilla met her aunt's gaze evenly. If she showed even a hint how everything was unraveling, Aunt Cordelia would insist on them leaving Shadows Fall without delay—and without a chance for Priscilla and Neville to reconcile.

Quietly she said what she had to say to avert any suspicions, "Neville is seldom swayed from what he plans to do."

Her aunt sighed. "That is true. You need to speak with him posthaste, Priscilla, for you are the only one he might heed."

"About what?" She was aware of Lady Barbara listening eagerly. "You know I have no intention of changing my mind about anything either." The lie was acrid on her tongue.

"I realize that you intend to marry this man, for you

have shown an uncommon lack of good sense on this issue." Before Priscilla could retort to the dual insult to her and Neville, her aunt continued. "The servants are whispering about him resuming the traditions of his family."

"Traditions?" She needed to know how much her aunt had overheard or pieced together.

"Do not act as if you do not know. He always informs you of his devilment." Opening another letter, she looked at it and, with a frown, put it on the larger stack.

"Which devilment is that, Aunt Cordelia?"

Instead of answering her, Aunt Cordelia looked at her friend. "Now do you see what I mean, Barbara? Not only is she besotted with him, but she is assuming his worst habits of talking around an issue in order not to give one a direct answer."

"Mayhap she does not know," Lady Barbara said, giving Priscilla a surprisingly sympathetic smile. "You know how men are, especially men of his ilk. They act one way with their families and quite a different way with others."

"Please do not insult Neville further," Priscilla said as she came to her feet. "You should trust me, Aunt Cordelia, to know that I would never bring anyone into this family who would have a detrimental influence on my children."

"Your first husband—"

"Was a vicar. What better influence could I offer my children than a churchman for a father?"

Lady Barbara chuckled. "She has a point, Cordelia."

"Will you speak plainly, Aunt Cordelia, of your concerns?" Putting her aunt in an embarrassing position with her friend would vex Aunt Cordelia further.

Her aunt smiled. "Priscilla, speaking plainly has never been a problem for you and me."

"No, so to tell me what concerns you about the Hathaway family traditions."

"They are illicit."

Priscilla laughed, because she knew that would be the response her aunt would anticipate. "Aunt Cordelia, you should not mistake Neville's rumored past with his current situation."

"I am not. My dear child, don't you know the truth of how the Hathaway family earned its wealth? Smuggling and wrecking."

"That *is* illicit."

"Is that all you have to say? It is being whispered that your future husband is assuming the leadership of a group of ragtag thieves and murderers, and you have nothing more to say?"

"I have much more to say, but it shall be to Neville."

Aunt Cordelia smiled triumphantly. "I thought you might feel that way, which is why I wished to speak of this to you." She patted Priscilla's hand. "You do have a good head on your shoulders. You simply need to use it more."

"Excuse me, Aunt Cordelia." She added nothing more as she glanced toward Lady Barbara, who had been listening in silence.

Her aunt's friend's brow was knitted, but she smiled when she realized Priscilla was looking at her. Priscilla waited for her to speak, but Lady Barbara said nothing.

Bidding both women a pleasant morning, Priscilla went out of the parlor. She climbed the stairs and went along the hallway to Neville's door. She was uncertain if he would speak to her after their harsh words in the middle of the night, something her aunt was sure to hear about soon.

The door opened as she raised her hand to knock. Her hope that Neville had been listening for her to arrive was dashed when she saw Riley's dreary face.

"Good morning, Riley," she said. "I would like to speak with Neville if he is awake."

"He is awake, my lady, but he is not here."

"Not here? Where is he?"

The valet shrugged stiffly. "I don't know, my lady. He was gone before I woke."

"Did he, perchance, leave a message for me?"

He opened the door farther. "I have seen nothing, but you are welcome to look."

Priscilla hesitated, feeling like an interloper going into Neville's private chamber when the echo of their angry words still hung in air. "He could not have gone far in his condition."

"That may be true."

She heard the valet's doubt, and she had to share it. Neville would not allow his injuries to keep him from doing what he intended, even if he hurt himself more. He had vowed to find Mr. Moyle's murderer, and he would do so, no matter what stood between him and his goal. She admired that about him, but it was that very aspect of him that was pushing them apart.

"Thank you, Riley," she said, turning to leave.

"May I ask where you are going, my lady?"

"To find Neville."

"May I ask where?"

"I would guess he is either at the shore or in the village."

"If you wish me to go with you—"

She smiled sadly. "Please stay here, Riley. If Neville returns before I do, send someone to let me know."

"I shall." He took a deep breath, then said, "Good fortune go with you."

"Thank you." She heard the door close as she went back along the hallway. It sounded so final.

A hand settled on his shoulder, fingers curving down his arm. Neville did not open his eyes. He wanted to stay within this dream where everything was as it should be and Priscilla had never looked at him with anguish in her eyes. Were those her fingers? He wanted to hold her as she melted to him, surrendering to the longings that consumed him.

"Are you asleep?" he heard her whisper.

How could she imagine that he could sleep when her breath glided along his nape and curved up behind his ear? Something silken brushed his face, and he thought of her in barely translucent drapes emphasizing her luscious curves.

"No," he murmured.

"Am I disturbing you?"

Yes! When you touch me, I cannot think of anything else. "No, of course not. Just thinking."

"Are you thinking of me?"

"Yes."

"Think of me always."

He frowned. Her voice sounded far away. He tried to open his eyes. The lids refused to rise.

"Think of me always." Her voice was disappearing into the distance.

"Priscilla!" he shouted, fighting to open his eyes. "Priscilla, don't go!"

"Think of me always. Think of . . ."

"Priscilla!"

At his own silent shout, Neville woke with a start to see Priscilla leaning over him. Not the Priscilla of his dreams, for she was dressed in a bright red spencer over her simple gown rather than in diaphanous robes. His head jerked up, and he started to put his arms around her to pull her closer. Pain riveted him. He groaned.

"Slowly," she whispered.

He appreciated that soft sound which did not add to the agony in his head. "Priscilla?" he asked, not quite sure if she was really beside him or if he was still dreaming.

"Slowly. You will catch your death of cold sleeping outside at this time of year."

"Outside?" He looked around and frowned when he saw the ruined temple. The motion sent more pain across his skull, but he ignored it. "Why am I in the mound?"

Priscilla sat beside him, adjusting a blanket she must have put over him. "I was about to ask you the same question. When I came in here, you were moaning and thrashing. It must have been quite a nightmare you were having." She drew her hand away from the blanket.

He wished she had not. Her gentle touch soothed the aches along him, muting the throb of pain. Taking a deep breath, he sat up. "It was a dashed horrible one."

"The way you were mumbling, I guessed you were under attack. That is why I shook you awake. I am sorry if I startled you," she said.

"I suspect my heart will start beating again in a day or two."

"What are you doing here?"

He searched his mind. The nightmare seemed clearer than his memories. "I was talking to Randall by the stone wall."

"Did you come here with him?"

"No, because he has left."

"Left?"

"Quit his position with the professor. From what he said, he could not tolerate the inconsistencies between what was being found on the beach and what was being found here."

Priscilla nodded. "I had seen that. When he left, I assume you came here to see if you could find an overlooked clue in Mr. Moyle's murder."

"That would be a logical assumption." Seeing her flinch as he said *logical*, he asked, "Are you all right?"

"As well as can be expected." She rose and brushed dirt from her cream dress.

"Why are you here?"

"I was looking for you. When I went to your room and Riley could not tell me where you had gone, I thought I should ascertain if you were going about in your rational mind or without it."

"And your conclusion?"

"None. I need to return to Shadows Fall. My aunt will be expecting me to continue to help her with plans for the ball." Dismay rippled across her face. "I have made every effort to keep her from discovering that it may not be held."

Pushing aside the blanket and coming to his feet, he ignored the agony careening down him. He took her arm before she could walk out of the mound. "Pris, you can pretend with your aunt that nothing is amiss, but we cannot pretend with each other."

"No, we cannot." Drawing her arm out of his, she

said, "I will not hold you to an offer you wish to recant, Neville. I love you too much to see you unhappy."

He took her hand and turned her to face him. His eyes focused on her lips. Those expressive lips, which with a single motion could reveal her fury or make him laugh at her observant words. When his finger swept a strand of her hair back behind her ear, he lowered his mouth toward hers.

"Help!" came a shriek. "Help me! Help me! Please, someone! Help me!"

"That is Professor Dyson," Priscilla gasped.

As he burst out of the mound with the best speed he could manage, Neville did not bother to tell her to wait where she would be safe. She would not stay put when the professor's hysterical voice resonated within the mound. When she ran past him toward the edge of the cliffs, he cursed his aching head and his eyes, which made him see ripples in the ground where there were none.

She disappeared down the cliff path, and he followed as best as he was able. He stumbled again and again. When he almost fell off the path, he slowed to a walk. He watched as she reached the bottom and raced to where Professor Dyson was on his knees next to—

Neville swore again, this time more vehemently, and forced his legs to support him as he lumbered across the stony beach. While Priscilla put her arm around Professor Dyson and tried to calm him, Neville stared down at the crumpled and broken corpse on the beach.

It was Oscar Randall.

TWELVE

While Reverend Mr. Rosewarne read the funeral service for Mr. Randall, Lord Beddlemere was alone in his family's pew. In the one belonging to Shadows Fall, Priscilla sat between Neville and Professor Dyson. The rest of the pews were empty.

Sunshine slipped through small windows on either side of the chapel, lighting only a couple of slabs on the stone floor. The simple stained-glass window behind the altar cast colors onto the embroidered altar cloth and candles. No light touched the coffin set in front of it.

Priscilla handed Professor Dyson another of the handkerchiefs she had brought with her. He blew his nose so loudly the vicar looked up, pausing in midword.

Rising at the end of the service, which was short because there was no eulogy, Priscilla was glad when Neville offered his arm. The discussion that had been interrupted by the professor's cries for assistance remained unfinished. With the first of the invited guests arriving late yesterday to attend the betrothal ball, she wondered when they would have a chance to say what remained between them like an invisible wall. It was odd not to be able to express her thoughts honestly to Neville, and she did not like it.

"You may send the bill for the gravestone to me,"

Lord Beddlemere was saying to the vicar when Priscilla emerged with Neville and Professor Dyson from the church. Wind whipped last autumn's leaves around the churchyard, but it was a gentler wind with a hint of spring in it.

"That is generous of you, my lord," the vicar replied. "Very generous."

"The man was working on my lands when he slipped off the cliffs." Drawing on his gloves, the marquess smiled sadly. "It is the very least I can do when I failed to have fences put up there at the beginning of the excavation work."

"Then he must have flown a good distance, because he was found below Shadows Fall," Neville said. His bruises were a ghastly purple, and one eye was almost swollen shut.

"Really?" The marquess laughed. "Then the cost of the stone belongs to you, Hathaway."

"What makes you think he slipped?"

Lord Beddlemere's smile became a frown. "Are you suggesting some sort of crime?"

"I am suggesting that when I last spoke to Randall, he was leaving the excavation site."

"He could have returned."

Neville shook his head. "He was planning to give you a look-in, Beddlemere. Did he?"

"Yes, but I was busy and could not receive him. He must have gone back to the excavation site."

"He had no plans to return. He was giving up his position with Professor Dyson."

"Foolish man!" choked the professor, blowing his nose again loudly. Blackbirds rose up with raucous protests at the noise. "He failed to see the truth in front of his face."

"Something many of us may be guilty of," Neville said quietly.

Priscilla was silent as she watched the men digest Neville's comment. Did he think one of the men here had had a hand in Mr. Randall's death?

Lord Beddlemere shrugged. "Who knows? The man may have angered someone in Trepoole and so been shoved off, but that is unlikely. He was not familiar with the cliffs, so he might have been hurrying too quickly down the path and fell to his death."

"He was," the professor moaned, "obsessed with looking for artifacts on the beach."

"Now you have two dead men," Neville said as he looked past her.

Priscilla was not surprised to see Constable Kliskey on the far side of the churchyard wall. He looked as if he had not slept in several nights, although his clothes were so wrinkled she also had to wonder if he had worn them to bed.

He apologized to the vicar for missing the service, then asked, "Professor, a few words with you if I may?"

"Me?" squeaked Professor Dyson. "I would not do my own assistant harm."

"No one is accusing you of anything," Priscilla said, offering the professor a comforting smile. "The constable wants only to ask you about anything you might have seen at the same time you discovered the body. Right, Constable Kliskey?"

"Yes, yes," the constable hurried to agree.

"I saw nothing out of the ordinary on the beach." The professor twisted a button on his waistcoat. "I had been looking for artifacts, so I was walking from one side of the cove to the other as I did with each receding tide."

Priscilla patted his arm. "I am sure Constable Kliskey would like to know as well who might have known that you make that walk twice a day."

Looking at the constable, who nodded, Professor Dyson said, "I cannot say for certain, my lady. Anyone who looks out the windows of Shadows Fall or Lord Beddlemere's house would be able to see me there."

"And from Trepoole?"

"Nobody comes out to the excavation from Trepoole. They are too busy with smug—" He looked with guilt at the constable, who was quick to glance down at the ground, appearing as culpable as the smugglers. "The people from Trepoole are too busy with their own business in their own snug houses."

Priscilla almost laughed at how relieved Professor Dyson appeared to be when he turned *smug* into *snug*. Could he honestly believe no one would take note?

"Don't you think," she asked, "Constable Kliskey would be interested to know if you saw anything near Mr. Randall's body?"

"He had a pack. It was filled with his clothes." He lowered his voice to a conspiratorial tone. "I searched them in case he tried to remove some of the artifacts."

"Did he?"

"No." The professor deflated as he owned to that.

"And you saw no one else while you traversed the cove?"

"Not until you and Sir Neville came down to the beach, my lady."

Priscilla looked at Constable Kliskey and gave him a warm smile. "Do not let me intrude on your questioning, Constable. No doubt, you have many, many more to ask."

"Yes, yes," he said as he had before, although he wore

a stricken expression warning that he had no idea what to ask next.

Thanking the vicar for the service, Priscilla went to the carriage from Shadows Fall. Neville lingered only a moment longer to bid Lord Beddlemere a good day before he came to hand her into the closed carriage.

Neville chuckled as the carriage drove away from the churchyard. "Pris, you need to have more sympathy for the barely competent constable."

"His questions would have been perfunctory at best. You saw how indifferent he was to Mr. Moyle's death."

"Because he is terrified of the smugglers."

"Maybe he is not want-witted, after all." She looked at his bruised face. "He may be smarter than you."

"I would be a fool to disagree with you on that." His smile faded when she did not return it. "I can fill your head with nonsense if you wish, telling you that I will change to be the man you believe you need for you and the children, but I thought you wanted me to be honest."

"I do want you to be honest, and I want to be honest with you."

"You have been." He clasped his hands between his knees. "I want to marry you, Pris. I would not have asked you otherwise, but . . ."

She nodded. He did not need to explain further. He had made his intentions clear. The decision was hers. She wished she knew what it should be.

"Is something wrong between you and Uncle Neville?" asked Leah as Priscilla closed the book she had been reading aloud.

Setting the book on the table beside Leah's bed,

Priscilla pulled the blanket up beneath her younger daughter's chin. "It is nothing that you need to be concerned about now."

"But you said less to him tonight than you did to Aunt Cordelia. Usually you two chatter like squirrels."

"Chattering squirrels? That is how I describe you and Daphne when you are being silly."

Leah sat up. "Mama, you are not answering my question."

"I did. You need not be concerned about Neville and me now."

"Are you planning on breaking your betrothal again?"

Priscilla sat on the edge of the bed. "Leah, you know that the first betrothal was only make-believe, an effort to save Neville from an overly attentive admirer." She had to smile as she recalled how Neville had suggested a betrothal as part of one of his most outlandish schemes. A scheme that had succeeded in uncovering the identity of a murderer.

"Oh." She considered that, then asked, "Is this one real?"

"Yes."

"So you will not break this one?"

"Leah," she said, "you are worrying yourself into a state." Motioning for her daughter to lie down again, she drew up the blankets.

"But I want Uncle Neville to become Papa Neville."

"Papa Neville?" Priscilla laughed in spite of the unhappiness plaguing her. "Have you mentioned that name to him?"

"Once, and he got a peculiar expression on his face. He either was very pleased or very displeased."

"I suspect a bit of both. He has been a bachelor for

many years, and hearing a name like *Papa Neville* is quite a change for him." She patted the blanket. "It is time for you to go to sleep." Blowing out the lamp, she said, "Sleep well, Leah."

Her daughter started to ask another question, but seemed to think better of it because she whispered, "Good night, Mama."

Priscilla went into the hallway before she released the sigh stuck in her throat. She must make a decision. How could she walk away from the joy she would have with Neville? How could she remain and know that at any time he might get into a situation he could not extricate himself from? She wished she had someone she could talk to, but her only confidant was Neville.

Going into her room, she undressed with her abigail's help. Glenda was silent, too, and Priscilla wondered what the servants were saying. They must have noticed the change. That did not worry her as much as their whispers reaching Aunt Cordelia's ears. So far, her aunt seemed oblivious to anything but the final preparations for the ball. Even though her aunt would have been thrilled to have the betrothal broken, if it had to be announced, Aunt Cordelia intended to have the very best, most memorable betrothal ball ever held in England.

When Priscilla had dressed in a nightgown and her dark blue wrapper, she thanked Glenda. Her abigail's good night was as soft as Leah's had been. Everyone in Shadows Fall was on edge, wondering what would happen during the night. Soon even the guests would take notice.

Priscilla brushed her hair before tying it back with a ribbon. She avoided looking in the mirror. Her own reflection might be laced with recriminations.

She started to climb into bed, then froze. A groan sifted through her window before being swallowed by the sound of the sea. It was the same groan she had heard before.

This had gone on long enough. Picking up the candle from beside her bed and pushing open her bedroom door, Priscilla went out into the hallway.

"Where are you bound?"

She wondered if she had ever been so glad to hear Neville's voice. Walking to where he stood in his doorway, she fought the yearning to touch the skin visible beneath the open front of his shirt. He was holding his cravat, so she knew he had been on his way to bed.

"I heard something," she said.

"And you were sneaking out to check?" He snarled an oath before adding, "Pris, you scolded me for being foolish and endangering myself to the point that I could leave you and the children mourning my death. What of you? Did you give a single thought to the children and me mourning *your* tragic death?"

She stared at him, not sure what to say.

"I did not think so." He tossed his cravat into his room and took her arm, steering her back toward her door.

"Neville, we need to investigate what is causing that groaning sound."

"We will. In the morning."

"But whatever is causing it may be gone."

"Then it will be gone." He reached past her and opened the door. "Pris, you cannot let the sound of the wind in the rocks convince you to do something stupid."

"It is not the wind in the rocks."

"If it is a manmade sound, we will find some sign of

who is causing it. Go to bed, and we will check in the morning."

She frowned. "This is not like you, Neville. You customarily are the first in line to check out anything."

"I have been doing some thinking." He scowled back at her. "You should, too, and mayhap you will come to your senses."

"Promise me that you will not go and investigate without me."

"I promise." He took the candle from her and put it on the table by her bed. "And you know that I never break any promise I make to you." He bent to kiss her, then stepped away, looking past her to her bed. His voice was unsteady as he said, "I should go before you persuade me to do something else witless."

"Neville . . ."

He cupped her cheek in his broad hand. "I told you that there is only so much a man can endure, sweetheart. I meant it."

She watched him walk away and wondered how many times she could endure letting him do that. The low, deep groan filled her room, but she paid it no mind as she closed her door and leaned her forehead against it. She knew the answer. She did not want him to walk away ever again.

The bruises on Neville's face seemed even darker the next morning. He had removed the bandage from around his head, and his hat was tilted at an angle so it did not brush the wound by his temple. As he and Priscilla walked around the north tower and toward the cliffs, the sound of carriages rattled from the front of the house.

"If I had not heard the groan myself," he said, "I would guess you had invented it to avoid standing in the foyer to greet the guests as they arrive."

"Nonsense," Priscilla said with a laugh. "I have been looking forward to welcoming friends I have not seen since we were in London at the end of the last Season. You have as well."

"I have been thinking fondly of some interesting games of chance at the card table." He frowned. "I shall have to devise some excuse to keep Beddlemere from playing."

She paused. "I know he is arrogant at times, but there are others attending who make him look as humble as a monk."

"But their pockets are not empty." He kept walking.

"What?"

He faced her. "Mr. Lampman, your neighbor on Bedford Square—"

"I know who Mr. Lampman is and that he arrived late last night."

"I had the opportunity to speak with him at breakfast, and he warned me that Beddlemere is living a life beyond his means."

"Those rents!" she gasped. "When he turned his tenants off his land, he lost those rents."

He nodded. "That is part of the problem. Beddlemere has a reputation for making foolish, costly wagers. I had not heard of it previously because we have no friends in common."

"Lady Barbara must not know."

"That is quite likely, for she is a woman who makes no secret of her desire for comfort in her life."

Priscilla looked back at the house. "I shall let Aunt Cordelia know at the first opportunity. She will want to

warn her friend. If—" She gasped as something rumbled under her feet.

"Are you all right?" Neville asked.

"Yes. Did you feel that?"

"Feel what?"

She pointed to the ground. "It seemed to shake."

"I felt nothing."

"Mayhap it is just here. Stand here." When she began
to step aside, he put his arm around her shoulders,
keeping her close to him.

With a gasp, she pulled back.

"What is it?" he asked.

She opened one side of his coat. "You have a gun with
you."

"I hope we do not need it for protection."

"Can you see well enough to aim it?"

"I can see far better than I could the time I was trying
to stop a light horseman in Westminster one night."

"Light horseman?"

He chuckled. "Low cant I should not have used. It
means a thief who prowls the Thames. Even though I
had been pummeled so fiercely the night before that I
had two black eyes, I had been sent by Bow Street to
stop him."

"Bow Street? You really worked for Bow Street?"

He held out his hand. "Some rumors about me are
true, sweetheart."

Slipping her hand into his, she wanted to thank him
for trusting her with even this small bit of his past. That
would embarrass him, and she did not want him to stop
opening up the doors to his life before they had met.

"Did you catch him?" she asked.

"Yes, both him and the two chaps who ambushed me.

They did not expect me to return." He looked around. "I still have not felt any quaking in the ground."

"Mayhap it was simply my knees knocking together."

"Unlikely." He led her toward the path down to the shore. "You are the bravest woman I have ever met, although you tried to persuade me last night that you are not the wisest."

"You were right last night."

His uninjured eye widened in mock astonishment. "Me? *I* was right? Certainly that is a cause for celebration."

"Don't be silly. You—"

His mouth over hers silenced the rest of her words. As he drew her closer, she stiffened. He started to step back, but she caught his arms.

"I want you to kiss me, Neville," she whispered, "but I do not want to hurt you."

"*You* can never hurt me with your kisses, sweetheart."

His kiss was gentle, and she was sure the brush of his cheek against hers brought him pain. Yet she could not edge away until he raised his lips from hers. She gazed into his eyes and wished she had never spoken the acrimonious words.

Again she wondered if he could sense her thoughts because he said, "As soon as we find out what is making that sound, let's walk over to the temple mound. That will allow us the privacy to talk about what still remains unsaid between us."

"I would like that."

"Even if Lady Cordelia chides you for being a bad hostess?"

"Even if she does."

Priscilla took his hand again as she followed Neville

down the steep path. They had only gone a few steps when the ground quivered again.

"I felt that!" Neville looked back at her. "Is that what you felt before?"

"Yes."

A moan rose in crescendo and dropped to a rumble.

"By all that's blue!" he gasped. "What is going on?"

As soon as they reached the shore, he paused. She knew he was waiting for another moan or another shaking. They did not have to wait long. The sound came from their left.

"It sounds like someone dying," he said as he motioned. "This way. It seems to be coming from there."

"Is that a cave?"

"It appears so." He peered into it. "There is enough light to go in a short way. Mayhap you should wait here, Pris."

"I don't want to meet the smugglers face-to-face on the beach."

"They should not be abroad in the daylight."

"If they are collecting their ill-gotten gains . . ."

"Come with me then."

That was what Priscilla had hoped he would say. Praying there were no beasts within the cave, she took Neville's hand and entered.

The sunlight began to dim after they had gone a few steps. Under her feet, the floor was smooth. She put her hand out to touch the wall, fearing it would be clammy. It was cool, but dry.

"The perfect place to hide wine from excise officers," Neville said. He bent down and ran his fingers along the floor. "There are scratches from where heavy crates have been moved across the stone. The Trepoole smugglers have used this in the past, although I doubt if they have recently with Professor Dyson stalking artifacts on the beach."

"Do you think that was why Mr. Randall was killed? Because that would keep the professor away while he mourned his assistant's death?"

Neville stood and wiped his hands. "That is a possibility."

"But what is causing the groaning sound?" She was tempted to turn around and leave before the smugglers decided to return. If she left, she was not sure she could convince herself to come back.

"Let's find out."

Easing one cautious step at a time along the passage as the light grew even sparser, Priscilla tried to breathe. Every breath wanted to cling inside her lungs, strangling her with fear of what could be lurking in the darkness. When another groan rushed down the corridor, sweeping over them, she fought her feet, which wanted to flee.

"We are getting closer," Neville said.

"But we are going to lose the light soon."

He put his finger to her lips. "Shh. Listen. Do you hear that?"

Priscilla strained and heard nothing but water lapping on the shore. No, the sound was not from outside. The water was in front of them.

When he drew her forward a few more steps, she realized it was not getting darker. It was actually getting brighter. She gasped when she discovered light coming from the right. Another passage must open onto the cove.

Water bubbled in a shallow pool in front of them. Neville squatted and took a handful. Drinking, he said, "It is sweet, so there must be a spring under the pool."

He stood and chuckled, the sound echoing oddly through the cave. "We should have expected to find one here once we saw the temple. This must have been considered a sacred spot."

She peered into the darkness on the far side of the pool. "Or the entrance to the underworld."

"That would mean the temple is dedicated to Pluto rather than the other god."

"All of this is fascinating, but what is causing the groaning sound and the ground tremors?"

"I see nothing that would cause either." He edged around the inky black pool. Running his hands along the wall, he said, "It looks as if someone has been working to widen this cavern or mayhap open it onto another." He pushed against some loose stones. They tumbled to the floor. "There may be a passage back here. With the skills the men in Trepoole have with mining, they could be digging more storage areas within these caves." He shoved against another large stone.

"Take care!" Priscilla called. "Take—"

A groan erupted through the cavern. It rose to a shriek that resonated off the walls, making them shake. Light flickered into the cavern. Light from overhead!

Her arm was seized, and she was yanked almost off her feet. She thought she heard Neville shout something, but her ears were battered by the shriek of shattering earth. Huge stones fell, breaking into pieces and splashing into the pool. Pain shot up her leg as he shoved her past the scree he had pushed aside. Blood burned on her shin, but she ran along the passage opening off to the side.

The ground heaved, and she fell to the ground. Neville pressed over her as a cloud of dust and debris exploded through the passage. The noise grew until she wanted to scream for it to stop. Mayhap she *was* screaming. She could not tell.

Then it was silent except for the sharp sound of a few last stones falling down against one another. She could hear her thudding heart and the rapid pulse of Neville's breath against her hair.

He sat and drew her up as she raised her head. She looked behind them to see a wall of stone. Even as she watched, water trickled between the rocks to stream along the passage floor.

"The roof must have fallen in," she said, gasping for breath and coughing in the dust.

"Not just the roof." He stood and walked closer to the stone blocking the passage behind them.

She rose, stepping around the water seeking a new way out of the spring. Lurching back to where he was looking up, she gasped in horror. She could see, through the gaping hole where the cavern roof had been, the torn wall of Shadows Fall. Atop the rock from the cave were the stones from another tower that had collapsed.

"I think," Neville said, "the smugglers may have a far vaster system of storage than we had imagined."

THIRTEEN

Priscilla had hoped she and Neville could sneak back into Shadows Fall without anyone seeing them. An unavailing hope, because as they walked out of the cave, Ennis was already on the strand. The footman blanched when they stepped into the sunshine.

"You were inside?" he choked, even though the answer was obvious.

Neville brushed stone dust and dirt off his ripped coat. "Get some men from the house. I want a fence erected here posthaste, so the guests do not take it into their minds to do some exploration. The roofs are unstable throughout the passages."

"All the passages?" Ennis's face became even more ashen.

"So it would appear." He continued to shake dust from his coat, as if getting it clean were his only priority. "Do you know the caves well?"

The footman shifted from one foot to the other and licked his lips before saying, "Every boy in Trepoole explores them at some time."

"A warning needs to be sent to Trepoole," Priscilla said. "The vicar should be able to warn the villagers that entering the caves again could be deadly."

"Both he and Tremeer from the tavern need to be

alerted." Neville grimaced. "This was my favorite coat, and I doubt it can be repaired." He looked up. "Why are you waiting, Ennis? Go and do as Lady Priscilla and I have ordered."

"Yes . . . yes, sir." He took a single step backward, staring at the cave's entrance, then another and yet a third before he whirled and ran toward the path leading up to the top of the cliffs.

Priscilla said in her most nonchalant voice, "It appears his knee has gotten better far more quickly than your face, Neville."

"So I noticed." He dropped the hem of his coat. "It would make one wonder if his knee had been hurt at all."

"He grew up in Trepoole, so he might have known the danger of wandering about here after dark. Faking an injury would allow him to avoid what you have suffered."

"That is one explanation."

"You think he is involved with the smugglers." She did not bother to make it a question.

"If he is not, he may be the only man in Trepoole who is not." He shook dirt from his hair and smiled. "Pris, you look like an old hag."

"Thank you. You have looked better yourself." She touched her bonnet's broken brim. "Being with you puts a great strain on my bonnets."

"I will have to buy you a new one when we return to London."

"More than one." Instead of laughing with him, she looked back at the cave. "Is your suspicion of Ennis's involvement with the smugglers why you lied about the state of the caves? The other roofs appeared quite steady and solid."

"It was in part a lie, but the new sections that have been dug may have undermined the whole." He took her hand and put it on his arm as they walked toward the path to the cliff's edge. "I hope all of Shadows Fall does not collapse into the earth. The house may need a lot of work, but having it vanish into the ground would be a drastic way of renovating it."

"The odors in the section near the east tower could have been coming up from the caves."

He nodded and smiled. "A good point about something I had almost forgotten about since Mrs. Crosby's efficient cleaning throughout the house. The smugglers may have had to remain in the caves for days if the excise officers were investigating. Their forced stay would have left offal behind."

As they reached the top of the cliff, several forms came rushing toward them. Leah was leading the way.

"Is it true, Mama?" she asked, panting from her run. She eyed them. "It *is* true! How could you?"

She smiled at her younger daughter. "It was not by our choice. We were simply in the wrong place at the wrong time."

"No! I mean how could you go to explore the caves without taking me?" She fired a glare at Neville. "You promised you would take me on an adventure soon."

"Soon," he said, "but not today." He draped an arm over her shoulder. "But *you* must promise me that you will not go into the caves now. It is too dangerous."

Leah nodded reluctantly. "As long as you take me on an adventure someday."

"That is a promise." He glanced at Priscilla and added, "It will be interesting, but not dangerous."

Priscilla wanted to thank him for setting those boundaries, but had no opportunity. They were surrounded by their guests, all asking questions without waiting for an answer. As the men drew Neville to one side in hopes of hearing details too exciting for the women's ears, Priscilla was herded toward the house by well-meaning friends.

She looked back and found Neville staring after her. Their gazes met for only a second before a tug on her arm warned her to watch where she was walking. She skirted the sheep droppings, but glanced back again. The brief connection between them was gone along with any hopes of discussing their betrothal. It could not be delayed much longer.

Knocking on a door in a recently cleaned section of Shadows Fall, Priscilla was pleased to hear Neville call, "Come in."

She had not been sure if she would find him in what Stoddard had called the book-room. Neville had been looking forward to the wagering that would fill the men's time until the betrothal ball, so it might already be underway. To call him away from the card table to have the conversation they must have would create a flurry of questions.

She opened the door to discover what once must have been an incredibly elegant room. One wall was covered with empty shelves behind glass doors, some of which were cracked. A grand window arched up toward the ceiling to offer a view of the field where Professor Dyson had been working.

Professor Dyson? Had anyone warned him about the dangers within the caves? If he decided to explore one, he could be killed. He must be told.

She heard the crackle of the fire on the hearth and

looked in that direction. In a mural, voluptuous nymphs and their muscular admirers, naked except for some conveniently placed drapes, were entwined in each other's arms. The mural continued around the room, each panel more erotic.

"Oh, my!" she murmured.

From the far corner, Neville laughed. "I missed painting over one."

"Intentionally?" She was surprised to see him without his coat. A black one was draped over a chair near the hearth.

He crossed the room and closed the door. "Unlike the other murals which were amateurish at best and, I suspect, painted by an ancestor with a lascivious imagination, the panels here were done by a talented artist. I could not bring myself to order them covered with paint."

"Draperies would conceal the more questionable panels without destroying them." She tried to look away, but her eyes kept shifting back to the scenes that would have made a rake blush.

"An excellent suggestion, Pris. I should have asked you to begin with." He tilted his head at a strange angle as he appraised the panels. "Don't you think that hanging from a tree while engaged in that activity would be impossible?"

With a laugh, she slapped his arm. She sat on one of the chairs facing the hearth, glad for the warmth and to have her back to the most outrageous panels.

"We have to talk," she said as he sat beside her on a low stool.

He stretched his legs out between hers and the chair. "I know." Looking up at the ceiling, he said, "I suspect there is little chance of that falling down to postpone the discussion once more."

"I would not be so certain of that after you have lost half the towers on this house already. There may be a honeycomb of tunnels beneath Shadows Fall."

"Stoddard has sent men to investigate the cellars. With my family's participation in smuggling, it is highly likely at least one tunnel emerges into the house." He leaned toward her, propping one elbow on her knee. "But finding tunnels is not what you came here to discuss, is it?"

"No."

"Pris," he whispered, folding her hand between his as he brought her to her feet, "say you have changed your mind and do not want to end our betrothal."

"I never have wanted to end it."

"If you need more time to consider—"

She kissed him, but drew back before she could add injury to his battered face. "No, I do not need more time to consider. I was a fool to say what I did, but I was so distressed by the sight of you so still and hurt."

"I cannot promise to outlive you, Pris." His broad hands framed her face. "There may come a time—"

Putting her finger over his lips, she said, "I understand, and I would be a fool twice over to let my fears of the past and the future ruin what we have right now. I love you as you are, Neville. Warmhearted and determined to make sure even the most downtrodden receive justice."

"And I love you as you are, Pris. Warmhearted and determined to make sure you help me gain justice for even the most downtrodden."

"Please make me the promise you made Leah."

"That I will take you with me on my adventures?"

"Yes."

"I will make that promise to you after we announce our betrothal."

"But not before? Why?"

He met her eyes steadily. "Because I will be meeting with the smugglers this evening before the ball begins. I cannot take you there. No women help bring the crates ashore."

"Why are you meeting them tonight of all nights?"

"The smugglers believe our betrothal ball is a diversion I devised to keep anyone from guessing my real purpose for coming to Cornwall. If I let the night pass without calling them together to announce the upcoming arrival of a ship, they will question the truth of my lies."

Priscilla had to own that made sense. "How long will you be gone?"

"I will leave at sundown, and I should be back before the first dance begins. The meeting is set for another cave I have been told about."

"Under another tower?"

He smiled. "I hope not." He clasped her hands. "Pris, after this, I will take you on all my adventures, although I cannot promise that, as I promised for outings with your children, all those adventures will be without danger." He teased the curve of her ear with a swift kiss. "After all, you are a dangerous woman."

"Me?"

He smiled. "You have presented a danger to my heart from the first time I kissed you."

"I do believe I kissed *you* the first time."

"Dash it! You are right, and that only proves my point that you are a dangerous woman." He smiled and reached for his coat. "It seems the time is overdue—"

A knock came at the door.

"I will be right back." Neville went to the door, opened it, listened, and nodded before he closed the door. He was only halfway to where she was sitting before someone rapped again. He gave her a wry smile and went back to the door. This time, he listened a bit longer before he nodded and said, "Have the section of the wine cellar cleared so we can get that door opened and see what is behind it, Stoddard, while the rest of the cellars are searched. There may be more than one entrance into the caves. Let me know as soon as the wine casks have been moved." He shut the door and came back to where she had sat again. "I assume you heard."

"Yes. Do you think the door in the wine cellar opens into the smugglers' tunnels?"

"It would have been convenient for the earlier Hathaways to bring their booty right into the house without having to take it aboveground." He smiled and arched a brow. "I collect you will want to be there when the door is opened or broken through."

"Without question."

"It might be just the escapade for Leah to participate in."

She shook her head. "I do not want her there. She is still young, and what has been left there by smugglers may not be something she should see."

"What are you expecting to find behind that door?"

"Expecting to find? I have no expectations, but I cannot keep from thinking of the people who have vanished. Those bodies must be somewhere." Her nose wrinkled. "That stench in the corridor near the east tower could be a sign to where they are."

His smile became grim. "You have as vivid an imagination as the artist who painted the mural in this room."

"Did you not have the same thoughts?"

"Yes, although we must keep reminding ourselves that finding the answer behind a door in the wine cellar would be dashed convenient."

Priscilla came to her feet. "A very convenient discovery at a very convenient time."

"There have not been too many convenient times lately." He slipped his arm around her waist. "A few when you have been close to me like this have been convenient, but those times seem to have been too long ago."

With a soft moan, she put her hand behind his head and brought his mouth to hers. She heard his breath catch. She savored the sweetness of the kiss, a sweet madness.

Another knock was set on the door. Neville murmured, "Ignore whoever it is. Mayhap they will go away." He bent to kiss her again.

The knock became more frantic.

"You should answer it," Priscilla whispered.

"I should, but that does not mean I will."

She laughed. "If you don't, I fear whoever is pounding on the door will break right through it."

Neville muttered an oath she doubted he intended her to hear as he went to the door. "What is it, Stoddard?"

The butler frowned at his sharp tone. "Sir, Lord Beddlemere and the constable have arrived at the house and wish to speak with you immediately."

"Lady Priscilla and I—"

"Lord Beddlemere was most emphatic, sir. He wishes to speak only with you."

Priscilla said quietly, "I have some guests to check on, Neville, so I ask you to excuse me."

"You do not need to leave, Pris. Beddlemere does not give orders at Shadows Fall."

Looking past him, she said, "Stoddard, please have the marquess and Constable Kliskey brought here to speak with Sir Neville."

"Yes, my lady."

As soon as the butler was out of earshot, Priscilla said, "Keep them away from the window."

"Why?"

"I am going to speak to Professor Dyson. He may not have been warned of the dangers in the caves."

"True. I did not suspect the professor was the guest you wished to check on."

She put her hand on the door. "Mayhap we should ask him to move into Shadows Fall. He may be a target of the smugglers, too."

"And you accuse me of doing dangerous things." He smiled coolly. "You are inviting the smugglers to turn their attention on Shadows Fall."

"You have already done that by asserting your rights as owner of this estate."

"Take a footman with you, Pris."

"I will." She smiled. "It appears exercising his knee has been good for Ennis."

Neville put his hand on her arm. "No, Pris. Take someone else. I don't trust Ennis. His so-called fall was even more convenient than finding that door in the cellar."

"All right." She heard footsteps coming along the hallway. "Your guests sound as if they are in a hurry to speak with you."

"I wonder what they have to say to waste my time now.

Did I tell you Beddlemere called yesterday to complain about the state of repair of the hedgerows between his lands and mine?"

She chuckled. "No. Is he afraid his sheep will come here and you will claim them for your own?"

"Who can tell with Beddlemere? Wish me luck."

"Good luck."

"Do not wish me good luck that way," he said, clasping her arm and spinning her back to him. He brushed her lips with his and whispered, "Wish me good luck this way."

"Good luck," she murmured, giving him a quick kiss.

"I am going to need more than that."

She met his mouth with her own craving for more. As her lips parted, he caressed them with his tongue before seeking within.

Her breath was ragged as she asked, "Is that enough luck for you?"

"For both of us." He smiled, and he cupped her cheek. "However, as you know, sweetheart, good luck is temporary. I will need more later." He winked at her as he walked past her to greet the marquess and the constable.

Priscilla stared after him. Later? She needed more *now*. More of his kisses, more of his fingers curving along her, his hard body pressed against her. Swallowing her moan, she walked in the opposite direction.

FOURTEEN

Leah insisted on going with Priscilla to where Professor Dyson was working near the cliffs.

"You cannot leave me out of everything," her daughter argued.

Suspecting Leah was as anxious to get away from her sister, who talked about nothing but the upcoming ball, as she was to have an outing, Priscilla acquiesced. She asked Stoddard to have a footman waiting.

"That is a fancy bonnet to wear for a walk in the fields, Mama," Leah said as she skipped along the upper hallway, unable to hide her excitement about visiting the excavation again.

"My everyday one needs to be repaired."

"Oh!" Her eyes widened. "Do you think we will face more peril?"

Priscilla wanted to say she hoped not, but she knew that would dishearten her daughter. "Who knows?"

"Daphne says Uncle Neville will save a dance for her at the ball," Leah said, bouncing on the steps. "Do you think he will save one for me, too?"

She smiled and wondered how she ever could have thought she would be happy without Neville in her life. He had been kind not to scold her for giving in to panic when she had feared he was dead.

"You have not been enthusiastic about your dancing lessons, Leah, if you recall."

"I know how to do some steps, and I will not step on his toes. May I ask him, Mama?"

"A young lady waits for the gentleman to ask her to stand up with him."

Leah rolled her eyes. "But, Mama, he may not know I want to dance with him."

Putting her arm around her daughter's waist, she said, "I will mention it to him."

It took longer than Priscilla expected to go down the upper stairs. She encountered several dear friends who asked her to have tea with them. Unable to tell anyone no, when she had been such a delinquent hostess, she invited them to join her in the parlor for a coze. Leah showed great patience, proving anew how happy she was to go with Priscilla.

When they reached the bottom of the upper stairs, a young man with light brown hair stepped forward and bowed. He gave his name as Angwin and said the butler had asked him to accompany Priscilla to the excavation site. She hid her astonishment at how young he was, for he could not be much older than Leah.

Priscilla tied her cape around her neck. "This will have to be a quick visit to the site, Leah, if we are to be back in time for tea. You may look about, but stay within sight at all times."

"I will not let myself get killed, too, Mama," she replied in a rather exasperated tone.

"See that you do not." She squeezed her daughter's shoulders. "Come along, Angwin," she added to the footman, whose face had lost all color at Leah's words. "I assure you that no one will end up dead today."

A screech raced through the hallway. Priscilla froze,

and Leah grasped her arm, her fingers digging deeply into Priscilla's skin.

"Lor', it is the specter of death himself, come to take a poor soul," moaned Angwin.

Priscilla was tempted to agree, but she said, "Nonsense. That is a very earthly voice."

"But who would be shrieking like that, Mama?" asked Leah.

"I shall go to see and—"

Another screech filled the hall, then lowered in pitch to become a furious voice saying, "You shall be sorry for this, Cordelia Emberley Smith Gray Dexter!"

"That is Lady Barbara," Leah said.

Priscilla had already recognized the voice and told her daughter to wait with Angwin by the stairs. Hurrying around the curve of the banister, she went to the parlor, the source of the loud voice.

She reached the doorway just as Lady Barbara snarled, "I saw you flirting with him."

Aunt Cordelia wore the expression that made even strong men cower, but it seemed to have no effect on Lady Barbara. "You have lost your mind. I have no interest in Robert Beddlemere. To own the truth, I find his cavalier behavior disagreeable. He is a duddering rake who thinks too highly of himself."

"How dare you speak so of Robert!" Lady Barbara's face was an unhealthy shade of crimson. Her hands shook by her sides, and her chin jutted toward Aunt Cordelia as she closed the distance between them until her nose was less than a finger's breadth from her friend's.

"Make up your mind, Barbara," Aunt Cordelia said in an exasperated voice. "First you accuse me of having a *tendre* for the silly man, and now you are scolding me for belittling him."

A sob burst from Lady Barbara. "I thought you were my friend, Cordelia."

"I am your friend."

"You have buried three husbands, and I have buried but two."

Priscilla had to put her hand over her mouth to keep a laugh from escaping at the idea of Lady Barbara being competitive about the number of late husbands her aunt had. Yet it was not funny, for Priscilla knew the pain of losing even one man she loved.

"Barbara, will you listen to yourself?" demanded Aunt Cordelia. "Who but a friend would stand here and listen to such skimble-skamble? Our friendship is why I have not put an end to this silly conversation by walking out of the room. I have no intention of trying to come between you and Robert."

"But his intentions are aimed at you, not me!"

"His intentions are something you must discuss with him, because I cannot speak of what he is thinking." She frowned. "Or not thinking."

Lady Barbara snarled, "You would like me to go and ask him, wouldn't you? Asking questions would make me look like a hysterical, possessive, jealous woman and make you look like perfection."

Priscilla had heard enough. More than enough, but she had hesitated, knowing she could not ask her aunt to stop interfering if she intruded on this quarrel. Motioning for Leah and the footman to remain where they were, she went into the parlor.

"Lady Barbara," she said, "you may not realize how far your voice is carrying. The openness around the stairwell allows your words to be heard throughout this section of the house."

"*I* have said nothing I am ashamed of."

Giving her aunt a sympathetic glance, Priscilla nodded. "I believed, Lady Barbara, you would like to know that a conversation you may have thought was private is quite the opposite."

Lady Barbara flounced out of the room in a high temper that would have earned a censure from Aunt Cordelia if any of her family had acted so. Leah and the footman moved back before Lady Barbara stormed right through them.

"Thank you, Priscilla," Aunt Cordelia said, coming to her feet.

Priscilla embraced her aunt, who was shaking. "You are welcome. I am sorry you had to suffer that."

"It was not your fault." Aunt Cordelia's voice regained its usual strength. "I fear the fact that Lord Beddlemere has not asked her to wed after all these years of her waiting for him to propose has quite undone her mind."

"She may be grateful that he never has made an offer for her."

"Why?"

She explained what Neville had learned about the marquess's financial straits. Her aunt listened and sighed.

"Barbara is, I fear, a foolish woman," Aunt Cordelia said.

"Should I send someone to sit with her?"

"I will go."

"You?" Priscilla was astounded. "But her rage is aimed at you, Aunt Cordelia. Mayhap you should give her some time to come down from flying up into the boughs."

Her aunt smiled. "I shall. By the time tea is ready to be served, she should be more of her customary self. Until then—"

Knowing she was risking sending her aunt into a pelter as fierce as Lady Barbara's by interrupting, Priscilla said, "I would like to stay and talk with you, but I have a guest who requires my attention, Aunt Cordelia."

"Of course, you must tend to your guests." Her frown returned. "In fact, I am very pleased to hear that you are. You have been absent too often."

"There have been many plans to make."

"And much mischief to become enmeshed in. I believe Daphne wanted my opinion on which jewelry she should wear to the betrothal ball." Her nose crumpled as if speaking the very words disgusted her.

Priscilla gave her aunt a kiss on the cheek and hurried from the room before Aunt Cordelia began to list anew the reasons why Priscilla was silly to marry *him,* as she referred to Neville. With Leah and Angwin following, she went out into the blustery day.

She looked toward the sea, where dark clouds gathered along the horizon. No one had confirmed if there were wreckers in the area, but they used stormy nights to lure ships to their doom. Mayhap the vicar would know. She would send him a note after returning to the house.

As they crossed the fields, Angwin cautioned, "Watch out for where the sheep have been. They graze through all these fields."

Priscilla was grateful for his advice as they picked their way through the field toward the excavation. When a parade of sheep crossed in front of them, she waited for the animals to pass, then waved to the lad herding them. He glanced at her, tipped his floppy hat in her direction, then scurried after his sheep.

It was a bucolic scene, but she could not shake her disquiet. Something was going to happen. Something she could not prevent because she had no idea when it might take place.

The wind stirred up the dried earth into miniature dust storms. Priscilla raised her cloak to cover her mouth and nose as they climbed over the stile.

"Over there, Mama," Leah said, pointing to the right. "Professor Dyson is over there."

"Thank you."

"Can I look about?"

"If you stay within my view." Priscilla looked at the footman. "And you stay with Angwin."

"Yes, Mama," she said grudgingly, but her smile returned like the sun bursting from the clouds as she added, "Angwin, you have to see what is in the mound."

"Leah . . ." Priscilla warned.

"I will not go inside unless you come inside, too, Mama. I promise."

Priscilla smiled as Leah skipped across the field with Angwin trying to keep up with her while still looking dignified. At a slower pace, Priscilla went to where the professor was supervising three men who must have come from the village. Their clothing was simple, their muscles honed from hard work.

Hard, illegal work, she suspected.

"Lady Priscilla!" exclaimed Professor Dyson as he noticed her. "I did not expect to see you on such a windy day."

"May I speak with you?"

He wiped dirt from his hands and his breeches. "Of

course, my lady. I always have time to speak to someone who shares my interest in the relics of the past."

"I regret that is not the reason I came to speak with you today."

As if she had not spoken, he said, "I miss Randall. I never had to check on his work as I do with the lads from Trepoole." He raised his hands and shouted, "Be careful with that spade! You could destroy something by driving it in the ground like that." He went toward the mound, motioning for her to follow. "I must show you what I found this morning."

"On the shore?"

"No, within the mound."

She hurried to catch up with him. "But I thought you had already explored the mound."

"A cursory exploration while I waited for someone to shore up the roof of the temple." He ducked into the mound and then came back out. "Look at this."

She took the pot he held out. "Oh, my!" She should say something else, but all she could do was stare at the red-painted pot. The art on it reminded her of the cup found on the beach. That had not been Roman. Was this? She ran her finger along the rim. Not a chip marred it. "This is amazing."

"It *is* amazing, isn't it?" The professor's chest swelled as he smiled more broadly. "It is my good fortune to find it."

"Yes, it is." The excavation site was becoming more confusing each day. Some good luck she could accept as a windfall. Too much was a whole different matter.

"Look!" Professor Dyson lifted the pot from her hand. "The figure on it is a woman. See the coils of her hair? She might represent a priestess." His voice grew hushed. "Or mayhap Juno herself. What do you think, my lady?"

"I think it is a wonderful find," she said when she saw his smile begin to wobble, "and you should bring it to Shadows Fall."

"Shadows Fall?" He frowned. "We have been storing the other things we have found at Lord Beddlemere's house."

She wondered why neither she nor Neville had asked about the artifacts' location before this. "I did not realize that."

"Lord Beddlemere is very fond of antiquities. He has many in his house that he purchased before travel to the Continent became dangerous."

"An avocation that must cost him dear."

The professor shrugged as he stared with wonder at the pot. "A marquess can afford such extravagances. In the past week, he has had an incredible stone sculpture delivered for a niche in his front hall. An athlete, I would assume, by the torso's muscles, but we may never know because the rest of the statue has been lost. It would have been costly, but what he paid for it means little when he can enjoy it in his home."

Priscilla did not contradict him, for it would be inappropriate to discuss Lord Beddlemere's financial difficulties with the professor.

"I am asking you to bring it to Shadows Fall, Professor Dyson," she said, "along with yourself. In the wake of the collapse of the smugglers' caves, both Sir Neville and I are uncertain how stable these cliffs are."

"But, if the cliffs are going to fall into the sea, I must secure what I can from here as soon as possible."

"And we are uncertain where the smugglers will next seek to hide their loot."

"Not my mound! They could destroy what is within it while storing their crates."

She nodded. "That is true."

"You must send some of your men to guard the mound."

"I cannot do that, for the smugglers have shown they are not afraid to kill. Do not forget Mr. Moyle and Mr. Randall."

"You think Randall was a victim of the smugglers?"

"I am considering every possibility, and you should do the same, Professor Dyson." She glanced at the men leaning on the handles of their spades and raised her voice so they could not fail to hear. "One possibility is that the smugglers will use this mound, and they will slay you or anyone else who tries to halt them."

The men dropped their tools and walked away without comment.

"They know what I am saying is true," Priscilla said as she motioned to Leah and the footman to come to where she stood. "You must return with us to Shadows Fall. With the many guests in residence now, you should be safe."

"Should be?" His face had no more color than the temple columns within the mound. Shoving the pot into her hands, he hurried to the stone wall. He picked up a canvas bag there and looked back to see if the rest of them were coming.

One problem was solved, Priscilla told herself as she held the pot carefully while she climbed over the stile and walked toward Shadows Fall. The others would not be as easy.

"My lady?" asked the footman as he fell into step beside her. Leah ran ahead to walk with the professor and ply him with questions.

"What is it, Angwin?"

"Thank you for not agreeing to have men guard the mound." He looked out at the sea. "None of us from Trepoole would be willing, and anyone else who said yes would be a fool."

"Are there any hints in the village about the identity of the smugglers' leader?"

His eyes narrowed. "My lady, it is said you know about Sir Neville's—"

"I am talking about the man who was leader before Sir Neville invoked his hereditary rights." She had to be careful what she said, even to those within Shadows Fall.

"No, there are no rumors."

"Nobody is curious?"

"Those who were are gone." He gulped. "Vanished, save for their ghosts that walk the shores on moonlit nights."

Priscilla nodded. The smugglers' leader ruled through terror, and she wondered how long he would wait until he proved that no one, not even a Hathaway, would push him aside.

Neville was sitting with his stockinged feet propped on a stool when Priscilla opened the door of the book-room and entered. She ignored the paintings on the wall as she went to his chair. When he did not stand, she did not call his name. He might be asleep. Rest would help him recover from his injuries.

"Don't tiptoe, Pris," he said without turning. "I am not in the land of nod, but I trust you will forgive me for not getting up."

"Are you feeling worse?"

"Much."

She hurried to his chair. "Is it your head that hurts?"

He hooked an arm around her waist and tugged her down onto his lap. When she yelped in surprise, he put a finger to her lips, then put his mouth over hers. She answered his yearning with her own. In his arms, it was possible to forget everything around them.

"Don't," she whispered when he raised his mouth. "Don't stop kissing me."

"I would like to keep kissing you, but my dashed head . . ."

Priscilla stood and went to another chair. Getting a pillow, she settled it behind him. "Lean back and close your eyes. That should help."

"Finding the answer to what in blazes is going on here would help more."

"I persuaded the professor to come to Shadows Fall." She lifted his feet and sat on the stool, setting his feet on her lap. Massaging them gently, she watched his eyes close with contentment, an expression she saw so seldom on his face.

"Good for you, Pris. Did he argue much?"

"Only that he fears for his precious excavation if the cliffs tumble into the sea."

He smiled. "You did not mention, I collect, that Shadows Fall would go with them?"

"I thought it unnecessary, especially when he did not ask."

"Good for you, Pris," he said again.

She hesitated, not wanting to disturb his rest, but realizing he must know what she had learned. She began to tell him what Professor Dyson had told her about Lord Beddlemere's collection. Neville's eyes opened, but he listened without questions.

"Either he has generous creditors," he said when she

was finished, "or he is obtaining the antiquities without paying for them.

"I wonder if he ever returned that flagon to the professor."

"According to the professor, all the artifacts that have
been found are being stored at Lord Beddlemere's
house."

"Now that is quite convenient."

She crossed her arms on his legs. "What did Lord
Beddlemere and the constable have to say to you?"

"If I were a gentleman, I would tell you that you do
not want to know."

"Don't try to protect me by acting as if I were nursed
in cotton, Neville."

"But you *were* brought up gently."

"Then I met you."

He chuckled and drew his feet off her lap. Leaning
toward her, he cupped her chin in his hand. "I like protecting you, Pris. I like it a lot."

"But you cannot decide now to be a gentleman. Tell
me what the two of them had to say. I am not a little girl.
I am not afraid of the dark, but I am afraid of what I do
not know. What I *need* to know. You cannot be standing
guard full-time on me and this house."

"Dash it! You are bothersome when you are right."

"So what did they say?"

Standing, he went to the window. "They came to
bring me a paper they had seen on the front gate of
Shadows Fall."

"That was nice of them."

He picked up an item from the windowsill. It glistened in the afternoon light as he held it up.

"That is a dagger!" she gasped.

"A dagger used to hold the page to the gate." He brought it back and handed it to her. "Look at the haft."

"It is made of tin." She frowned. "Who would make a haft of such a soft material?"

"A man who had access only to tin."

"One of the men in Trepoole who has worked in the mines?"

He nodded. "That is an assumption anyone would anticipate us making."

"But you think it was someone else who put the knife in the gate."

"Yes." His face tightened, revealing every sharp angle.

"The leader of the smugglers?" When he nodded again, she asked, "Why?"

"Because of this." He reached under his coat and withdrew a piece of paper. Unfolding it, he handed it to her.

She read aloud, " 'Beware. Next time, Pluto will destroy you along with the caves.' " She held it out to him. "Neville, it is not like you to be distressed by such a threat to you and me."

"Not to us." He tilted her hand so she could see the back. "To your aunt."

"Oh, my!" she breathed when she saw her aunt's name written in blood red letters. "She will not like this."

"Nor do I. Protecting your aunt will not be a simple task, because she will cause such a hullabaloo that she would give any assassin ample opportunity to slay her."

"But we must protect her."

He sighed as he took the page and folded it again. "It seems we must."

"You need not sound so reluctant because Aunt Cordelia is the target."

A quick smile tipped his lips. "You mistake my reaction, but your aunt will not if I warn her."

"I can tell her."

"And mention that I showed you this note?"

It was Priscilla's turn to sigh. "She may ignore it simply because you are connected with it." Squaring her shoulders, she said, "There is only one thing to do. We must have the servants join us in watching over her."

"The servants we can trust."

"Yes, not the ones from Trepoole." She closed her eyes. "It is not in my nature to distrust people when they have done nothing wrong."

He enfolded her to him as he whispered, "But at least one of them has, Pris, by leaving this note on the gate. The only question is which one. The smugglers' leader is determined to drive us away from Shadows Fall with ever more dangerous pranks."

FIFTEEN

Priscilla stood behind the curtains in the minstrels' gallery. The dust woven into the fabric threatened to make her sneeze, and she twitched her nose in an effort to dislodge the sneeze silently.

The guests were dancing in the hall below while the trio of violinists played a quiet melody that was almost lost in the huge space. She could not delay going in to meet their guests much longer.

She scanned the room and saw her aunt talking to a man and a woman she could not identify from this angle. She did recognize Stoddard. The butler was standing right at her aunt's elbow as he had pledged he would. A footman Neville had brought with him from London—Gordon was his name, she remembered—was lingering an arm's length away, his head slowly turning back and forth as he watched for anyone intending to do Aunt Cordelia harm.

Where was Neville? He should have returned to Shadows Fall before the first dance. That had been more than an hour ago. She did not want to imagine something horrible had happened, but she was uncertain what else would have delayed him.

"Mama, what are you doing here?" asked Leah as she slipped into the gallery.

"Checking on the gathering before I go down."

Her younger daughter sat on a padded bench, grimacing when a moldy odor rose from it. "Is that what a hostess should always do?"

"Either check herself or send a servant in to reconnoiter for her. That is an odd question for you to ask. I would expect it from Daphne."

"I am curious." She ran her hand along the stone wall beside her. "Someday, I may be holding a betrothal party of my own in a grand house like this."

Priscilla bit back her groan of dismay. She had not launched her oldest into the Season, and Leah was beginning to envision her own future. The girls were growing up too fast, but nobody had ever found a way to slow children on their journey to becoming adults. How much longer would it be before Isaac began to think of females as something other than someone to torment with silly pranks? All too soon, the three children would be leaving for good to make their own lives.

Tears filled her eyes as she clasped the ring she wore under her gown. How proud Lazarus would have been to see the children now and how much he would have enjoyed being present when they took marriage vows and welcomed their own children into the world.

Now Neville would be at her side, exasperating and challenging and loving her and the children as if they were his own. They loved him as well. And so did she, although she was ready to strangle him for being late for his own betrothal party.

"Where is Uncle Neville?" Leah asked, and Priscilla guessed her daughter would not be the only one asking that question.

"He had some business to attend to before the ball."

Leah sat straighter. "With the smugglers?" She slashed

an imaginary sword. "Do you think he would let me go and watch them bring crates ashore?"

"Most certainly not! That is no place for you."

"But he took Isaac when he went to the surgeon-anatomist's laboratory."

"Something he will not do again." Priscilla recalled her anger at Neville for letting her son accompany him to such a disgusting place. Isaac had enjoyed every minute of it, and he had spoken often in the past six months of that episode.

Folding her arms in front of her, and resembling her great-aunt for one astonishing moment, Leah scowled. "It is not fair that Isaac has all the fun just because he is a boy and the earl."

"Isaac is tending to his lessons while you are here," she reminded her daughter gently.

Leah's smile returned. "That is true, but I would like to watch the smugglers."

"They do not like to be watched."

"I know, Mama. That is why it would be so much fun to see them bring their booty ashore."

"They are not bringing anything ashore tonight. Promise me," she said, taking her daughter by the shoulders, "that you will never go to watch for them on your own."

"Oh, Mama!" She pouted for a second, then giggled. "I have just the jolly. I will get Uncle Neville to take me."

"Not tonight."

"Not tonight," she agreed, looking out at the room below. "Tonight I want to watch the betrothal ball. You will remember to come and get me for the announcement, won't you?"

"I would never forget something or someone that important." She gave her daughter a hug before going back out into the hallway.

Her smile vanished as she saw Neville's door remained open. Bother! She could not argue that finding the murderer was important, but he should have sent her word that he would be delayed so she could have a plan to explain his absence to their guests . . . and her aunt.

"Riley?" she called.

The valet stuck his head out from the bedchamber. "Here I am, my lady."

"I am assuming Neville has not returned."

"Not yet." He looked about ready to weep. "I have had everything ready for him for several hours."

"You know how Neville is." She should not have come here. She often ended up consoling the valet on the difficulties of serving a baronet who had interests unlike any other gentleman.

Knowing she could not delay any longer, even though the guests would be astonished to see the bride-to-be without her fiancé, she reminded herself that nobody expected anything commonplace from her and Neville. She went to the ballroom, adjusting her lacy gloves. Not even Aunt Cordelia could find fault with Priscilla's appearance tonight. Her light blue gown with a delicate ruffle at its hem was of the latest fashion, and her silk slippers shimmered in the light from the three lighted chandeliers.

"Where have you been, Mama?" asked Daphne as soon as Priscilla entered the ballroom.

The chamber had undergone an incredible transformation since the first time she saw it. The floors were swept and glistened from being polished. Although bright light cascaded down from the center chandeliers, the walls were hidden in dusk. Chairs were set closer to the middle of the room, so the guests who chose not to dance would have places to sit and enjoy conversation. The chairs also kept the guests from wandering through the darkness, a precaution aimed more at protecting Aunt Cordelia than preventing a clandestine rendezvous.

"Mama?" Daphne's impatience came out in the single word.

"I was waiting for Neville."

"Where is he?"

She put her hand on the shoulder of her daughter's unadorned white gown. "Where he is presently is not a topic to be discussed now, Daphne."

"Oh." Her eyes grew large and round. "Aunt Cordelia has been looking for you."

"Why?"

Daphne recoiled, and Priscilla knew her question had been too vehement. "She has been anxious that you have not arrived as she says you should have."

Priscilla relaxed a bit. Her aunt's reaction was so comfortingly customary. "Do you know where she is?" She looked around the crowded ballroom. "I see Lady Barbara."

"Then Aunt Cordelia is on the side of the room farthest from her." Daphne pointed. "There she is. She is by the orchestra, Mama."

"Where?"

"With Lord Beddlemere."

The phrase Priscilla thought of saying would have shocked those who would not believe a parson's widow knew such words. She would not speak them aloud, but they fit this situation. Lord Beddlemere's interest in her aunt was an unneeded complication this evening, most especially when Priscilla was uncertain of his level of involvement with the smugglers.

"Wait here, Daphne."

"But, Mama—"

"Wait here for Neville. He should be arriving at any time."

Daphne brightened. "And then I can dance with him."

"Yes." She gave her daughter a smile and edged around the dancers.

If Neville was right, and she had every reason to believe he was, Lord Beddlemere might be interested in her aunt's fortune. It was odd to think of a marquess as a fortune hunter, but that was the one valid explanation for him setting aside a woman who had waited patiently for so many years for him to propose. The other she could imagine was far more abhorrent. He had brought the note to Neville. Could he have written it himself? She wished she had thought to ask Neville his opinion on that.

"Where have you been, Priscilla?" demanded Aunt Cordelia in the same tone Daphne had used. "Your guests are beginning to talk about the fact neither you nor *he* have been seen in the ballroom."

"Neville has been delayed, and I decided I would be inhospitable to wait any longer." She forced a smile. "Good evening, Lord Beddlemere. I wanted to tell you that you were kind to bring the message on the gate to Neville."

The marquess, who was dressed as finely as if he expected to be presented to the Prince Regent, could not hide his astonishment. "I had no idea he would tell you about it."

"There are few secrets of consequence between

Neville and me." Her smile became sincere as she realized that was the truth. "Do you honestly believe the threat to be genuine?"

"Yes. That is why I have stayed by Cordelia's side."

"What threat?" asked her aunt.

"It had to do with some ancient Roman gods," Priscilla answered, trying to sound flippant. "I think it was another prank like the snake in your bed."

Aunt Cordelia shuddered and wafted the lacy fan matching her green gown in front of her face. "Please do not remind me of that horrible event."

"You are showing a great deal of bravery, my lady," Lord Beddlemere said, frowning at Priscilla. "Bravery or foolishness."

"Either way, there is nothing I can do about it tonight." She gave him a broad smile. "After all, tonight I am about to announce my betrothal. Why should I allow anything else to intrude on my happiness tonight?"

"Priscilla," her aunt said, "do speak with *his* butler. He is hovering over me as if he expects me to take ill at any moment."

"I will, Aunt Cordelia, but you must blame me for his attention."

"Excuse me?"

She lowered her voice and leaned toward her aunt. "I told him he should take his cues from you because you are far more familiar with events like this one than I am." She wished she could be honest with her aunt, but the uproar might create even more trouble and give whoever wrote the threat the very chance he needed to kill Aunt Cordelia.

Her aunt smiled. "Priscilla, you are beginning to show some signs of wisdom." She turned to Lord Beddlemere. "I do have to own Priscilla was a fount of strength when someone used that accursed serpent to frighten me."

Leaving Aunt Cordelia to regale the marquess—at length, Priscilla suspected—about the horrors of finding a snake in her bed, Priscilla walked back toward the door. A slight nod in Stoddard's direction was the only acknowledgment she could give him. She appreciated his steadfast guarding of her aunt. She saw Daphne standing at the door, looking wistfully into the corridor as she waited for Neville to arrive for their dance.

Where was Neville?

Three hours later, Priscilla had no answer to that question. She had slipped out of the ball twice and found Riley waiting with growing anxiety in Neville's room. She had not gone again because she did not want to distress Daphne more.

When Stoddard approached her to ask if he should have the wine to be used for the toast after the betrothal announcement removed from the ballroom, she said, "Yes, take the wine back to the kitchen."

As the butler started to bow his head, her aunt pushed past him with uncharacteristic gaucheness.

"Priscilla," Aunt Cordelia said, "you cannot send the wine back without some explanation to your guests."

"We are not having the announcement now as planned."

"You must tell them that. There is already too much gossip about where *he* is."

"His name is Neville, Aunt Cordelia."

Her aunt's eyes widened. "I know that. Why are you telling me that?"

Answering the unanswerable, because her aunt clearly did not realize how she always avoiding speaking of Neville by name, would be a waste of time. Her aunt was right. Priscilla must say something.

Aunt Cordelia followed—along with Stoddard trailing after her aunt—as Priscilla walked to the stairs at the back corner of the ballroom. From there, she could call for her guests' attention. She stepped up on the first riser and faced her guests. She had not needed to worry about getting their attention. Every eye in the room was aimed at her.

With a smile, Priscilla said, "First, I want to thank all of you for making the long journey to Shadows Fall to honor the Hathaway family tradition of announcing betrothals in this room." She had no idea if there was such a tradition, but nobody would be able to contradict her. Not even Neville would know.

The guests exchanged glances, and she knew they were wondering why Neville was not with her. She wished she had an answer for them. More important, she wished she had an answer for herself. Neville had told her he would return in time for the first dance, and he was always a man of his word.

"I know," she continued, "this is the time when Neville and I should be announcing our betrothal. Unfortunately, his arrival has been delayed by some important business here at Shadows Fall." She forced a laugh and was pleased when it sounded almost natural. "Therefore, the announcement will be at breakfast on the morrow. Thank you for understanding."

As she stepped down from the riser, a buzz of whispers raced through the room. The guests, she knew, were speculating about what business would keep a man from the announcement of his own upcoming wedding.

She was, too.

* * *

Priscilla woke at the creak of the door opening. The candle on the table beside her had burned almost out, so its light did not reach across Neville's book-room. She had come here in hopes that Neville would find her and Aunt Cordelia would not.

When had she fallen asleep? After the debacle of the betrothal ball, she had been certain she would pace the room all night. Too many nights with too little sleep had left her so exhausted she had not been able to keep her eyes open.

Light flashed, stunning her. She saw an arm holding out a dark lantern that had been opened enough so its light shimmered off a pistol's barrel.

"Pris! Thank heavens, you are all right!"

She looked past the gun to Neville's taut face.

"And Lady Cordelia?" he asked.

"Mrs. Crosby and Stoddard are taking turns guarding her room." She jumped to her feet. "Where have you been?"

"In gaol."

"Gaol?" she gasped.

He set the lantern on the table next to the sputtering candle. "The good constable decided to do something about the smugglers. He brought men to ambush me with a knock to my skull, which seems to be the way to dispatch one's enemies along this shore."

"Like Mr. Moyle and Mr. Randall?"

He touched the back of his head gingerly. "They chose only to knock me senseless. When I woke up, I was in a cell."

"But you are here now."

"I got out."

"I can see that. How?"

His smile was predatory. "Pris, you know I learned a few skills when I lived far less grandly than I do now. Picking a lock was one of them. The cell's lock was astonishingly simple to open once the constable fell asleep."

"And where is Constable Kliskey now?"

"Still asleep." He struck his fist against his hand. "He shall not be waking up for several hours yet."

"Oh, Neville, you are going to be in so much trouble for attacking a constable."

"Not as much trouble as he shall be for locking up an innocent man without cause." He held up his hand to halt her reply. "All right, an almost innocent man."

She laughed. "You are incorrigible."

"I believe you have mentioned that before." He undid his cloak and tied it around her shoulders. "We have to go, Pris."

"Go? Where?"

"Kliskey ambushed me after I had a chance to see where the smugglers were bound for our meeting. Their meeting place needs to be explored further."

"Now?"

"I gave them enough tasks to keep them busy until dawn or until they sober up from the ale I arranged with Tremeer to have waiting. Having a tavernkeeper as an ally is never a bad thing." He grew serious as he added, "I promised you, Pris, that I would take you with me on all my adventures after the betrothal ball."

"After we announced our betrothal is what you promised."

Darkening the lantern, he blew out the candle. He took her arm and led her through the room as if he could see like one of the banished cats. His voice was a husky whisper as he said, "This is close enough to what I promised."

"You are going to persuade me, Neville, that you truly are a gentleman."

"No doubt I shall do something in short order to disabuse you of that notion."

"No doubt." She held his hand as they went into the corridor. "And, to own the truth, I assumed you announced our betrothal."

"How could I announce a betrothal when my fiancé was not present?"

"I assumed you would figure out a way."

"And the guests assumed that you had figured a way out of our betrothal."

He drew her close to him and pressed his mouth over hers with a fire as fierce as what burned in his eyes. "Why would anyone believe I want a way out of our betrothal?"

"You will have to ask them at breakfast before the actual announcement."

"Breakfast? Dash it, Pris! You picked a most inconvenient hour. I have been busy most of the night."

"That will teach you not to show up at our betrothal ball next time."

"There will not be a next time. We are going to be married for the rest of our lives."

The warmth from his words stayed with Priscilla as she slipped with him down the stairs and toward the back of the house. She asked about the door found in the wine cellar, and Neville told her that it opened only to another storeroom.

"A dead end," he said.

"Please choose another phrase."

He smiled as they slipped out of the house. He clung to the darkness along the cliff. There was no moon to light the way, but the stars' faint glow helped a little. He led the way down the path, warning her to be careful. At the bottom, he turned to the right rather then to the left where the other caves had been. He put the pistol under his coat and opened the lantern just enough to allow a finger of light to escape.

Priscilla had dozens of questions, but she asked none as Neville led her along the strand. He must be certain the smugglers were elsewhere because he did not caution her to keep her steps light. The stones clicked together beneath his boots until he paused in front of a cave at almost the opposite side of the cove from the other one they had explored.

She looked up at the cliff. "We must be close to the temple mound."

"Right beneath it, I would guess."

"Are they connected?"

"I have not seen any signs of it . . . so far." He held up the lantern. "Watch your step. Once we get a few yards in, there are crates everywhere."

Priscilla followed him along the passage, which narrowed with stone that had fallen to the floor. When she grasped his hand holding the lantern and aimed the light up the wall, there were no signs of raw rock where the stone had broken away as in the cave with the spring.

"Someone has gone to a lot of work to make this cave look as if it has fallen in," she said.

He chuckled. "And here is all the proof we need that smuggling is a profitable business in Trepoole." He focused the lantern's light on the floor.

She stared at more crates than she could count. "Are they all filled with wine?"

"No, several crates contain lace and silk." He rubbed her skirt between his fingers. "Mayhap even this silk came from here. This way. I want to show you something else I discovered after I sent the men on their way."

"More?"

"Much more." He led the way to opposite wall. The boxes here were smaller. He opened one and lifted out a cup. "Do you recognize it?"

She examined it. "It is the twin to the one Professor Dyson and Mr. Randall found on the shore."

"There was room in this box for both cups." He picked up the crate and turned it over to reveal broken slats. "It appears the other fell out."

"Why didn't it break?"

He shrugged. "Mayhap the box was sitting on the shore and broke when it was picked up to be brought here. That would have left the cup to be found." He set the box back on the others. "These are filled with antiquities."

"Lord Beddlemere!" she gasped. "He must be sneaking them into England."

"That makes no sense, Pris, although I am sure Beddlemere is involved up to his ears in the smuggling."

"Do you think he is the smugglers' leader?"

"I would not be surprised, but I have no proof. However, he does not need to sneak artifacts into the country. Half of the great houses in England are filled with art and antiquities bought during grand tours on the Continent."

"If he wanted to hide his purchases from his creditors, he might . . . No," she said, negating her own thought. "That makes no sense either."

He reached in another box and lifted out a glass jug.

"How beautiful! Professor Dyson has found nothing like this at his excavation."

"I wager he would have."

"Do you think someone is planting antiquities for him to find?"

"I think Beddlemere is. I simply cannot understand why. He could take these and put them in his house and no one would be the wiser. There is some aspect of this that we are still missing. Let's keep going along this passage. We might find the answer farther in."

"Neville—"

He shouted. Light struck Priscilla's eyes, then sprayed the ceiling. She gasped as the light disappeared. Stretching out her arm, she found only empty air.

Neville had vanished.

SIXTEEN

"Neville?" Priscilla wanted to shriek his name, but she feared alerting whoever had attacked him that he was not alone. She could not see anything. Anyone could be hiding among the crates. Panic caressed her, urging her to surrender to its frigid fingers. "Neville? Where are you?" She paused, listening. She heard no one else. If he had not been ambushed, then . . . She called a little louder, "Neville? Answer me! Where are you?"

She took a single step in the dark and tripped over a box. Her left shin burned, and blood glided down her torn stocking. Taking a shuddering breath, she crept on hands and knees toward where Neville had been.

Her hand dropped into nothing. Gripping the edge of the cave's floor, she inched forward. She pulled back and could not halt her shriek when light blasted her eyes as it had when the phantasmagorical intruder prowled through her bedchamber. The sound rang against the rocks overhead.

From below her, she heard, "Pris! Are you all right?"

Neville! It was Neville! He was alive, and he must still have the lantern.

"Neville? Are you down there?"

"Where else would I be?" came back a hushed answer. Its very matter-of-factness was comforting.

She peered down into a vast hole to see Neville standing at the bottom. He had fallen far below, and she knew he could not climb out on his own. Something reeked. She hoped it was just some small dead animal putrefying below, but feared it was not.

"Are you hurt?" she asked.

"Not bad. A few more bruises to add to my collection. How about you?"

"I am fine." A scraped shin was nothing to concern either him or herself with now. "What stinks so appallingly?"

The light shifted, and he cursed. "This may be where the missing men vanished. There are several corpses down here in very sorry condition. Some of them are wrapped in canvas which has come open. Stones are spilling out." He swore again. "I suspect they were supposed to wash out to sea and sink, but, from the looks of them, a recent storm sent them back up on shore. That is not the only very interesting thing down here."

"What do you mean?" When he lifted the lantern, she saw more crates. They were a different shape from the ones on the level where she knelt. These boxes were longer and narrower. "Neville, what is in them?"

"That is what I intend to find out. I hope it is not what is stenciled on the sides. Hold this." He stretched as far as he could and held up the lantern. "Take care you do not fall, too. The edges of the hole are thin. It appears from the marks on the ceiling down here that the room was recently made higher. Too high, for they cut too close to the floor above. Hold the lantern over the opening, Pris."

Lying on her stomach and reaching down, she was just able to grasp the handle of the lantern. She gripped the handle with both hands as the lantern shook.

Neville glanced around the space and picked up two rocks. He slipped an end of the flatter one beneath the top of the crate. Pounding upward with the other stone, he began to force the crate open.

She looked over her shoulder, although she could not see anything in the darkness. The noise echoed through the cave.

"Hurry," she urged. "Someone could hear."

"I know," he said through gritted teeth. "There. That should be enough." He dropped the stones and slipped his fingers beneath the raised lid. Shoving upward to the sound of protesting nails, he lifted it high enough to peer in.

At his curse, Priscilla asked, "What is it?"

He pulled something long and shiny from the crate. Grease dripped from his fingers. "A gun. One of many."

"Gun? To arm the smugglers?"

"I suspect not."

"Are you suggesting the smugglers are involved in sneaking weapons into England? That makes as little sense as the antiquities up here."

"Both make a great deal of sense, Pris, if you consider the weapons are being smuggled *out* of England, and Beddlemere is being paid with those valuable artifacts."

Priscilla could not speak. Smuggled weapons could have but one destination. They must be going to France to be used against English soldiers. Fury welled up in her. The marquess was fulfilling his craving for art without a regret that he was sacrificing brave English men.

"Pris!"

At Neville's call, she shook herself. Her anger was wasted unless she let it fire her determination to halt the smugglers. She asked, "How could all the men of Trepoole be traitors?"

"Most of them probably cannot read, so they would not know what was in the crates. I am sure Beddlemere has spun them a great tale. Pris, get something I can use to climb out of here." He shoved the gun back in the crate and used his fist to hammer the lid back in place.

Putting the lantern by the edge of the hole, Priscilla looked around the floor. A length of rope was sitting atop a crate. She pulled and discovered it was caught beneath the crate. Raising her foot, she shoved against the box, which barely moved. She bent, put her shoulder on the side of the crate, and grunted as she tried to push it aside. Again it hardly moved, but when she tugged on the rope, it came free.

She lashed the rope around the box, yanking on it to test the knot. Satisfied, she turned to toss it into the hold. She froze at the sound of footsteps. She wanted to warn Neville, but even a whisper might alert whoever was coming toward them. Neville had a gun, but she was defenseless. Blowing out the lantern, she crept behind the stack of crates holding the antiquities and peeked around them.

She flinched when another lantern's light bounced closer. The man's face was lost in shadow, but not the gun in his hand. He held the lantern higher, revealing his face.

Ennis! She clenched her hands so tightly that her nails drove into her palm.

The footman called, "Sir Neville? I know you are here."

Priscilla looked around in desperation. Ennis would see the hole in the floor soon. She needed a weapon. But what? She had to stop the footman from killing Neville. Reaching carefully up into the uppermost crate, she picked up the glass pitcher and hefted it. She would have only one chance.

"Sir Neville!" shouted Ennis. "I have Lady Priscilla here, and I will shoot her if you do not—"

She leaped out. Raising the pitcher, she smashed it against his head. He crumbled to the ground. Shards surrounded him and crunched beneath her feet as she picked up the rope. She picked up his lantern and gun. Running to the hole, she called to Neville.

He appeared from around the crates of guns and caught the rope as she tossed it into the hole in the floor.

"Thank goodness, you did not believe him!" she said as he tugged on the rope to test it.

"He has not been honest before. I did not think he would be now."

She watched the rope go taut and kept her eyes on Ennis to make sure he did not wake up.

"Don't shoot," Neville said as he climbed out.

Priscilla looked at the gun she held. Lowering it, she asked, "How do you fare?"

"I have been better." He kissed her swiftly, then hobbled toward the footman.

Ennis groaned and shifted, and she pointed the gun at him.

Neville pushed the gun aside as he tied the footman's hands and feet with the rope that was still lashed to the crates. Shoving Ennis over onto his back, he slapped the footman's cheek to rouse him.

Ennis's eyes narrowed with fury as he looked up at them, but his eyes grew wide again when he stared at the gun Priscilla was handing Neville.

Pointing the gun at the footman's head, Neville said without emotion, "Tell me what you know."

"Sir Neville, I never intended to hurt anyone."

Neville laughed sharply. "I did not ask your intentions. I asked you to tell me what you know."

Priscilla wrapped her arms around herself and stepped closer to Neville, glad she was not the one being interrogated by him. She watched emotions flicker across the footman's face, all fleeing to leave only terror.

"He will kill me if he learns I told you," groaned Ennis.

"I will kill you if you don't."

When Priscilla gasped, Neville scowled at her. She bit her lip, knowing she must not allow her heart to persuade her to plead for mercy for Ennis. These men would offer no clemency to Neville or her or her family.

Ennis must have understood Neville's threat was real, because he began to talk. Through the scarcely coherent babble, she picked out that, once he had been hired to work at Shadows Fall, he was given orders to portray the phantom haunting her in an effort to scare them into leaving. He had pretended to be hurt so he could avoid the trap waiting for Neville on the shore.

"It was another warning," Ennis said. "We thought you would leave then and not try to take the leadership of the smugglers from Lord Beddlemere." He blanched.

"You are not telling me anything I don't already know about Beddlemere," Neville replied. "Save for where he is right now. Why isn't he here himself?"

"A marquess does not inform a footman of his plans."

Neville pressed the tip of the pistol against Ennis's skull. "But you are not really a footman. You are his strong arm whom he sent to slay me. He must have realized I knew the location of this cave because Kliskey did not find me soon enough. Tell me what you know."

"All I know," whispered the terrified man as Neville's thumb settled on the hammer, "is that he plans to put an end to your interference tonight. He sent me here and he went to Shadows Fall."

"Aunt Cordelia!" gasped Priscilla. "He is going to kill Aunt Cordelia as the threat said."

Picking up the lantern, Neville handed it to Priscilla. "Let's go. We have not been here very long. We can still halt him."

She rushed with him out of the cave, ignoring Ennis's shouts not to leave him trussed up without any light. She tried not think of what he feared in the darkness. Nothing could be more horrible than the evil hidden behind Lord Beddlemere's smile.

When she saw Neville was limping, she asked, "Can you make it back to Shadows Fall?"

"Do not waste time with ridiculous questions," he growled. "What other choice do I have?"

Slipping her arm around his waist, she helped him climb the steep path. She was afraid they would be sent careening down the path, but somehow they made it up the cliff. He lurched against her as they crossed the field. The house had never looked so far from the cliff's edge.

The closest door opened into a corridor running near the kitchen. As they hurried along it toward the main stairs that were the quickest route to Aunt Cordelia's room, Neville glanced at the blood staining her gown and gave her a sympathetic smile. She was glad he did not slow.

He stopped so abruptly, she ran into him, knocking him forward a pair of steps. He put out his arm to halt her, but she could not move as she stared at Lord Beddlemere lying facedown in the center of the foyer. The floor was speckled with red as it had been when she arrived, but she knew this was not paint. Blood trickled from a dark hole in his coat.

Neville ran to him and put his hand on Lord Beddlemere's back. "He is alive!" He flipped him over roughly. When Priscilla began to protest, he frowned at her. "He is a dead man anyhow, Pris. Whether he dies from the ball in him or at the gallows, what does it matter?"

"Neville, what a horrible thing to say!"

"I am just repeating what he said about Moyle."

Before she could do more than gasp, the marquess groaned and opened his eyes. "Stop her," he choked.

"Her?" asked Priscilla.

"Barbara. Stop her from killing Cordelia."

Priscilla stared at Neville in horror. Had he harbored any suspicion that the threat to her aunt had been written by Lady Barbara? The thought had never entered her mind.

Even limping, Neville took the steps two at a time. He was halfway up the second set by the time Priscilla reached the bottom. By the time she got to the top, she heard a door slam against a wall. Another door opened almost into her face, and Leah stepped out.

Priscilla gave her daughter a sharp shove back into the room. "Stay there, and don't come out until Neville or I open this door." She shut the door in her daughter's startled face and ran toward her aunt's room.

She halted in the doorway and stared at an unbelievable sight. Lady Barbara was aiming a gun at Aunt Cordelia, who was crouched on her bed, while Neville was putting the pistol he carried on the floor.

"Kick it away," the lady ordered.

He obeyed, kicking it under a table.

"Help me," groaned Aunt Cordelia. "Don't let her shoot me."

Lady Barbara's face became hideous with her rage. "You deserve to die. Both of you." She gave a laugh. "I wager you believed Robert was in charge of the smugglers, didn't you, Sir Neville?"

"It was a safe assumption, or so I thought," he replied calmly as he folded his hands behind him. One finger crooked to motion Priscilla closer. "Are you saying *you* were the one who came up with the idea of smuggling guns to the French?"

Aunt Cordelia gasped in horror. "Sweet saints! Your own nephew was killed by a French ball on the Peninsula."

As Priscilla edged nearer to Neville, Lady Barbara said as if she had not heard Aunt Cordelia, "Foolish Robert was interested only in collecting his dusty fragments. I took a larger view. When this war is over, more markets for English wares will open. Why not let Napoleon's coffers finance my enterprises? I hoped to become richer than King George himself."

"But Beddlemere negotiated for antiquities rather than gold," Neville said. His hand reached up beneath the back of his coat.

"And he brought that foolish professor here to provide a screen. Beddlemere could display his relics without anyone being suspicious. His elaborate scheme failed."

"When Moyle started stealing the artifacts and Randall began to question the authenticity of the site and how the artifacts got there"—he lifted something out of his waistband with his right hand while he motioned again to Priscilla—"he killed them." He held out his left hand, palm up.

Hoping she understood what he wanted, Priscilla did the same, pressing her left hand against his back so he would know what she was doing.

"Then," Lady Barbara said, her voice becoming shrill, "he wanted to share everything I had helped him get with another woman." She took a step closer to Aunt Cordelia, who cowered back against the headboard of her bed. "You! He wanted to share it with you!"

As Lady Barbara stared at Aunt Cordelia, Neville slipped his hand from beneath his coat and put his pistol in Priscilla's hand. The one under the table must be Ennis's. She touched his back again to let him know she had it. Turning it in her hand, she hoped she would not have to fire it at Lady Barbara. She did not know if she could save her aunt in time. Behind her, she heard heavy, slow footsteps, but she did not dare turn. She waved away anyone who was stupid enough to come close. They needed to have a route to escape in case Lady Barbara decided to fire the gun toward the door instead of the bed.

"So you decided to get rid of him," Neville said.

When Lady Barbara looked at him, Aunt Cordelia sagged against the headboard. Priscilla tried to give her a bolstering smile, but it was impossible. They could not guess what the madwoman would do next.

"Why should he," Lady Barbara screeched, "be in charge of the smugglers when I knew how to use these witless natives to the best advantage? *I* will become the leader of the smuggling gang."

"The men will never accept a woman as their leader," Neville said calmly.

As the footsteps came closer, Priscilla motioned more frantically for everyone to stay back.

"They will accept me, or they will die." She laughed. "After all, who suggested to Robert the best way to dispose of those who tried to gainsay us? Letting them rot in the sea!"

The footsteps finally became silent.

"I did not want to kill you, Cordelia," Lady Barbara said, her voice breaking. "I thought you would leave when I put that snake in your bed. I thought you would go when I left that note for you."

"Note?" whispered Aunt Cordelia. "What note?"

"Didn't you see it?" The gun trembled in her hand.

"Now!" Neville shouted, reaching for the pistol Priscilla held.

Other fingers closed around it. As she was thrust aside, she cried, "Lord Beddlemere!"

The marquess raised the gun as the circle of blood on his waistcoat widened. "Get out of my way, Hathaway!"

Neville started to turn. "Don't, Beddlemere."

The marquess gave him a fierce shove back. Neville leaped toward Aunt Cordelia. Both guns fired as he pushed her off the far side of the bed. The window behind the bed shattered, but Priscilla stared in horror at Lady Barbara. Crimson stained her gown as she reeled back and collapsed. In the doorway, the marquess toppled over. Neither made another sound.

Priscilla jumped over Lord Beddlemere and ran to her aunt's bed. Scrambling up on it, she looked over the side. "Are you hurt?"

"Not much worse." Neville stood, wincing, but helped her aunt get up from the floor.

Flinging her arms around her aunt, Priscilla whispered, "I am so glad you are alive, Aunt Cordelia! I am sorry we did not guess Lady Barbara's threats were real."

"Why should you?" asked her aunt. Her voice held no more than a trace of its normal confidence. "*I* did not realize it, and I have known her more years than I wish to recall."

Priscilla watched as Aunt Cordelia turned to Neville. Right now, her aunt was grateful to him for saving her, but in the days and weeks to come, Priscilla guessed Aunt Cordelia would be vexed that she owed Neville her life.

"Thank you, Neville," Aunt Cordelia said. "There are times when the low skills you learned in the past prove useful."

Trying not to laugh at the backhanded compliment, Neville said, "It was my pleasure, Lady . . . " He grinned. "*Aunt* Cordelia."

Her aunt scowled.

EPILOGUE

Neville stood and held up his glass of wine. The guests gathered in the ballroom paused in their discussions about the extraordinary events that had happened earlier this morning in Shadows Fall. Most had been woken by the sound of pistols firing, and a few had gone to watch Ennis herded out of the cave by excise officers. No one missed seeing Reverend Mr. Rosewarne arrive to oversee moving Lord Beddlemere and Lady Barbara's bodies to St. Anthony's in Trepoole. It was the greatest irony that, in death, Lady Barbara had guaranteed that she would always be with her lover.

"Family and friends," Neville said as he smiled at Priscilla, who was sitting next to her daughters, "I am sorry I was not able to join you last night as promised. Some of you may have believed I was questioning my decision to ask the most fascinating woman I know to marry me. Some of you have questioned my sanity in even having a ball and the announcement of a most important event here at Shadows Fall. I trust you will now understand the truth about both."

Priscilla slowly came to her feet as Neville put down his glass and held out his hand to her. When she put her right hand on his, he shook his head with a smile.

Taking her left hand, he drew out a small case. He flipped it open.

She gasped as she saw a pearl and sapphire ring on the velvet inside the box. "That is the ring in so many of the Hathaway family portraits."

"All the portraits of the women who were want-witted enough to marry a Hathaway baronet." He lifted the ring and placed it on the fourth finger of her left hand. "*This* is why I came to Shadows Fall and wished to hold the betrothal ball here. I needed time to look for this ring—the servants assured me it must be here. I want you to wear it so the world can see that you have agreed to marry me, Pris." He held her chin between his thumb and forefinger. "You will be my wife, won't you, Pris?"

"As soon as possible." She barely heard the cheers and applause from their guests because Neville pulled her into his arms. His kiss told her that *as soon as possible* would not be soon enough.

AUTHOR'S NOTE

Nothing ever goes easily for Priscilla and Neville. Not even wedding plans or firing of Priscilla's daughter Daphne into the Season. Planning to wed as soon as the banns are read, Priscilla and Neville find themselves caught up in theatrics of a different sort when the corpse of a wealthy woman is found at a theater where Neville once was an actor. Could one of his friends be the murderer? But why would an actor want to murder his rich mistress?

As death stalks the theater and the *ton,* Priscilla and Neville must uncover the murderer's identity before their wedding plans come to a tragic end. Look for *The Wedding Caper* in June 2004.

Readers can contact me at: P.O. Box 575, Rehoboth, MA 02769, or visit my web site at: www.joannferguson. com or send an e-mail to jo@joannferguson.com.

More Regency Romance
From Zebra